THE CORRECTED LORE OF
A FAMOUS PHILANTHROPIST

DUSTIN PERRY

ILLUSTRATED BY AARON WOLF

Printed in Australia

First Printing: August 2021

Shawline Publishing Group Pty Ltd
www.shawlinepublishing.com.au

Paperback ISBN - 9781922594273
Ebook ISBN - 9781922594280

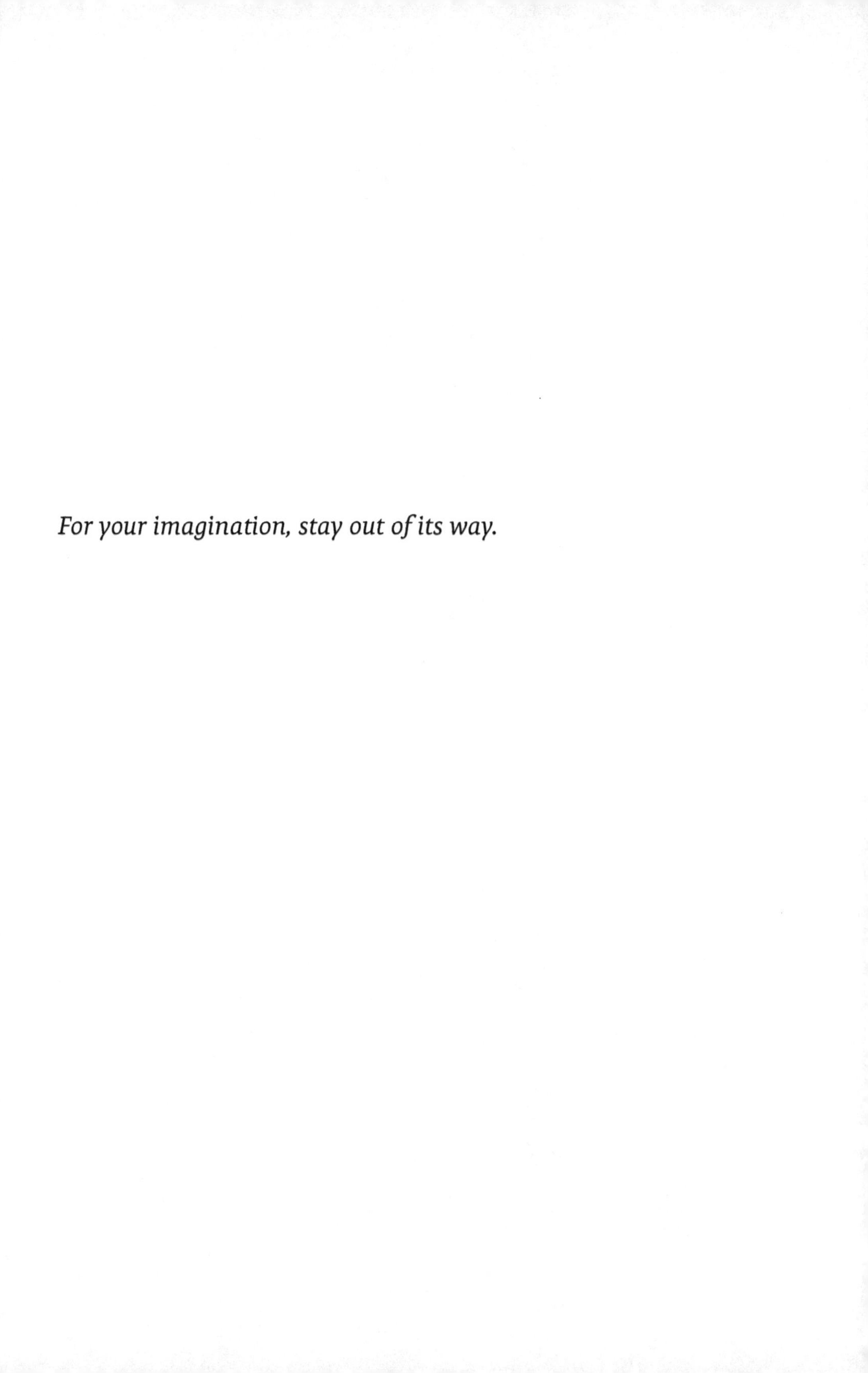

For your imagination, stay out of its way.

1

It had been happening for years.

All around the world, on the night of December 24th, homes would be filled with both fear and excitement before a loved one was lost. Neither the parents nor the kids could control what was about to happen. They could only hope, and if it was their thing, pray the night went well for their family; neither of which were much good as a strategy.

But the hopes held for this night were very different for kids compared to their parents, as were the stakes if the night didn't go as they hoped.

Failure to receive a requested present was a far more desirable failure than losing a member of the family, but for one family each year this was the tragedy that would forever define Christmas for them.

Krampus was the name of the man responsible for this misery, though I remain unsure whether it's more accurate to say man or beast, as it was never settled which he was more of.

You're about to learn a lot about the story of Christmas, and though their roles are very different in reality, many of you will be shocked to learn the main characters are real, including Dasher, Dancer and the rest of that group you know so well, though it may surprise you to learn those are the names of elves, not reindeer.

There has always been some disagreement about what came first – Krampus and the annual attacks, or Santa and the gift giving.

The answer is simple, and I'm not going to try spinning this like the fairy tale ver-sion; if you're happy living in a land of rainbows and butterflies, perhaps this story's not for you. The fact is that Krampus came first. Forget the rumours and old tales; take it from me. That's the way it was for many years; Krampus was the only one sneaking into homes the night before Christmas.  Nothing good happened the night of December 24th, it was just fear and worry.

As the number of attacks added up year by year, Krampus' power increased in a gradual but certain path toward becoming what you may call a god. A horrible evil god. He sought this power, and he wanted it all, so he could destroy it all. Everything. You, me, the mountains, the rivers, the shops and the theatres; anything that might make people happy.

But as the years passed and more loved ones were missed

by more families, the growing power of Krampus became impossible to hide, and the great elvish wizard Rudolph went to Santa with fearful concern. Like many patterns, once attention was drawn to it, it became very clear, and questions were asked about how everyone had missed it for so long. Santa and Dolph saw what was happening, and they stepped in to stop it.

They set out immediately, using Dolph's spells and Santa's presence to keep the kids of the world safe from Krampus attempting to add to his toll on that special December night. Santa patrolled the world and visited each individual child, making Krampus' plans not impossible, but very difficult for him to continue.

Santa's first Christmas visits were nothing more than this. No presents or surprises of any kind were involved for a long time, and it was only later at the insistence of the always thoughtful Dolph that Santa began including gifts as part of the service.

'You're kidding, aren't you? Come on Rudolph, do the police deliver presents?' he had responded in a half serious tone when Dolph first suggested the idea, but he was easily convinced with the offer of increased magical assistance to carry the extra workload.

This ran smoothly for a very long time, and Krampus seemed to have been put off to the point of not having been sighted for many years, and the disappearances stopped, with even the risk of them forgotten by many. People were happier, safer. - Life was better.

2

The night the Christmas Philanthropist Project failed; Sophie White was taken. But unlike the many taken before her, she had a chance. Krampus had managed to narrowly miss Santa's arrival at the White's house by a few seconds, but what he wasn't able to plan for was Sophie's big brother Aiden. He saw the kidnapping and followed them out the front door, which didn't bother Krampus at all; the image of a child chasing after a being of his size and power almost defined futility in his mind and he left, with Aiden standing screaming after them on the front lawn.

What he didn't consider however, and what this *futile* attempt did achieve, was filling the void of time between the moment of the kidnapping and that of Santa's arrival, and Krampus was very quickly in a rage at himself for not killing the brother on the spot, as the chase was now on.

Aiden had only witnessed the abduction of his sister because he had been out checking for Santa, hoping to get a look at the magical man all the kids looked up to like some kind of generous superhero. He was certainly surprised when he saw Santa, but he didn't give it the thought he would have if he had caught the man coming down the chimney. He just saw someone to help his sister and ran toward him yelling, 'You've got to help me, a man just took my sister.'

Though he instantly had terrible concern for this little girl and knew exactly what had happened, Santa was encouraged by the fact she was still alive, and that there was a witness, which he had never heard of happening before. One side of the mythical man's mind was shocked and concerned Krampus was back, and wondered why. And the other part was studying what he knew to be different; it wasn't a smooth and traceless disappearance this time like they used to be. Had the beast become sloppy and without fear of being seen? Was he slipping with age and lack of practice? Or did he just no longer care for sneakiness and mystery like he used to?

There was a lot to think about and a lot he didn't know, but he needed no more convincing to take action. He reached over the side of the sleigh and grabbed a fist full of Aiden's dressing gown from the back of his neck and easily lifted him in, dumping him on the floor at his feet without the sleigh coming to a complete stop. Then they were off again, rolling Aiden onto his back as he lost balance in the fast and sharp rollercoaster like turns.

He shouted and said words Aiden had never heard in his life as he waved the dark leather reins about, and the sleigh swayed and bumped around, like the air they were flying through was full of bumps and holes; much less gracefully than he imagined Santa's sleigh might travel.

After a couple of minutes, he gained both the steadiness of foot as the flight began to level out, and the courage to pull himself up to a careful kneel before moving onto the front seat. His priority was to look for his sister, and though he couldn't quite see her, he could see the machine in front of him she was taken in, and he was surprised to now notice it was also a sleigh; though certainly not one as nice as this one. It looked old, dirty, and probably stolen.

He looked sideways at Santa, who held out a hand, inviting him to shake it. 'I'm Santa.' he said.

The first thing Aiden had noticed about him was he was quite unlike the mythical character that was apparently very loosely based on him. There was no big belly or cute button nose, but instead this six foot six Viking, as Aiden's mind labeled him, looked more like a professional athlete than anything even slightly potbellied. Rather than cute or button like, his nose looked as if it had been involved in more than a few fights, with a bend that had been knocked into a zig zag shape and back again. He wore a couple of gold rings on his thick tattooed fingers, and hard callouses covered unusual parts of his hands. From there, up over the collection of worn and dirty bracelets on his wrists, was enough hair to think there may be a bit of werewolf in him too, which of course there was not. Though he certainly stood on powerful legs, he seemed to be top heavy with his broad shoulders and barrel chest tapering off to a thin and more aerobic looking waist.

The long red coat partly fit the description most would

give for what they call Santa, going to just below his waist, over the top of black pants and a very thick leather belt that was just as much for protection and carrying weapons as it was for keeping his pants up. The coat wasn't the clean, bright red you imagined. It was a filthy damaged piece of barely red leather; the sort of red you only know is red because I told you it used to be, and it had a tiny tuft of the white fluff lining hanging out through the ends of the sleeves, which was also filthy. There were none of the cotton wool like fluff balls from the movies, no weird sleeping hat, and he was never clean or particularly cheerful.

'Yeah, you are. You're real.' Aiden replied.

'Yes, I do feel quite real,' he agreed, then looked at Aiden and paused before going on 'Well, use your manners boy, aren't you going to introduce yourself?'

Aiden felt a bit embarrassed by this. 'Oh, I'm her brother. I mean I'm Aiden White.' he stuttered.

Reminded of the issue up ahead, Santa looked away from him and put his concerned eyes back on the dark sleigh in front of them and took both reigns in one hand so he could vacantly stroke his beard with the other. 'Yes, you're her brother,' he said distantly as he stared up ahead through the dull moon light. 'What happened?'

'I don't know, I didn't really see much. I just came down the stairs as she was getting dragged out the door, and I heard her trying to scream, but it sounded like he had his hand over her mouth or something. I ran out the front door after them and just saw this giant of a man, even bigger than you, with this weird mask on, throwing her into that.' He finished, pointing at the sleigh up ahead.

'Hmm.' was all the reply he got, unless the beard stroking also meant something.

'Hmm, what?' Aiden spoke back, frustrated at the lack of explanation. 'Who is he, and what's he doing with Sophie?'

'Sophie. Beautiful name,' he said in a quiet voice like it was to himself, then looked at Aiden. 'I don't know what to tell you, I thought this was over a long time ago. Sophie is the first taken in 163 years.'He then went through the history books of his mind explaining the story of Krampus, finishing with how he had overcome the evil sequence and become the delivery guy he is best known as today, and replied with, 'Well, I'm more than just a philanthropist.' when Aiden commented on his shock at Santa not being just the Christmas gift giver.

He'd started the night with a plan to sneak out of bed and try to catch Santa dropping off gifts, but he was doing this to prove to himself the guy didn't exist, and it was really his parents putting presents under the tree every year, not because he actually expected to see him. Starting from there, he went to meeting the man himself in a sleigh flying over the town in pursuit of his kidnapped sister. He would have been surprised to find the Santa story to be true at all, and to now find he does exist, but the story had been way undersold, Aiden didn't know what to think. He was so confused.

He turned to Santa and looked him up and down. He seemed quite relaxed as he sat with the reigns hanging slack in his hands, watching the dark sleigh ahead of them. The distance between them was shrinking, which was great, but Aiden wondered what was going to happen when they caught up.

He was quietly impressed with this version of Santa, who was much fitter than the potbellied one in the stories, and certainly looked like he spent some time in the gym; a very athletic looking Santa. He could feel the big man looking at him out of the corner of his eye, which made him feel sort of uncomfortable, but continued to examine him anyway, and it was now he started to believe this guy may be quite capable when this chase turned into a fight. There was a shield strapped to his back, which Aiden hadn't noticed before, as it was well hidden in the same dark red as his worn looking coat. The handle of a sword was sticking up from within the shield by Santa's thick neck, and the smaller but matching handle of a knife sat out on the top of his right boot.

3

'What's the plan when we catch them?' he asked, pointing up ahead to the other sleigh, still getting closer.

'Yeah, good question. I'm working on that right now, buddy.' Santa replied, which slowly leaked away some of the confidence Aiden had in him.

They both sat quietly for a minute or two and just looked blankly ahead, then Santa spoke again, 'Don't worry about it, I'll just pull up next to them and jump across to his sleigh then take her back.- It'll be fine.'

'Oh wow, I'm feeling really good about this.' Aiden replied sarcastically, really worrying that Santa was a bit too casual about it.

As reckless and poorly planned as it may have seemed, that was the plan they went with, and as they approached the dark and dirty sleigh and bumped in beside it, Santa's casual confidence actually had Aiden starting to believe it could work.

Aiden was so happy to be close enough to see his sister, and able to send shouts of 'It's going to be ok' and 'We've got you', as he saw her tear-soaked eyes look to him with fear. Being this close also gave him his first good look at this horrible being called Krampus.

He wasn't quite fat, but he just didn't seem as fit as Santa, though undoubtedly strong, with the thick build of a weightlifter. Even from a few metres away, Aiden noticed his strange skin that looked somehow hard and dirty, on a level that may possibly have never been washed. His clothes were damaged and patched together, and he held a thick pointed bar for a weapon.

'A bit closer.' Santa mumbled, but just as he was tying off the reigns, getting ready to jump sleighs, there was a scream, a bang, and the whole thing shook to the side, forcing him to abandon the jump. He drew his sword as he turned around, pushing Aiden to the ground for protection as he went, then turned his sword on a gargoyle who was lunging toward him, as a group of them swarmed the sleigh.

They were wild looking creatures with dark blue skin, wings growing from their upper backs, and muscles on their muscles. They weren't bird wings, but some horrible sharp dinosaur like wings with incredible power that was of great use for both flying and fighting. They were armored, but only in the most vital of places, and though they held weapons, they carried themselves in such a way that told Aiden as soon as he saw them, they would have no problem fighting with their bare hands.

Santa took out the first one with a swift burst of well targeted energy, but the second was on him immediately, followed by a third. He traded blows of his sword for lashes of the creature's sharp claws, before he quickly realised he couldn't beat this thing in a test of strength, and he ducked the next swing and used its momentum against it. Taking a fast and firm grip on its arm, grazing the blade-like claws on the way past, he threw himself backward, pulling it onto him, and used his legs to kick the creature over his head and out of the sleigh.

Springing back to his feet and looking around for Aiden, who was still crouched on the floor at the front of the sleigh, Santa took one step toward him, then felt claws latch onto his shoulders and lift him into the air. It was only now he realised the obvious; throwing a gargoyle overboard achieves nothing; they are gargoyles; they fly. He took a blind upper-cut at the head he knew was somewhere above his, and he connected hard with all the strength and effort he had avail-able, and it loosened its grip enough for him to bend forward and flip it over his head onto the floor in front of him. This time he thought it through a little more, and kept a tight grip on one arm, twisted it as it hit the floor, and put all his weight into it, leaving it too injured to use.

Aiden sat up and stuck his head above the side of the sleigh in the direction of his sister. 'They're getting away,' he shouted at the struggling Santa.

'Yeah, I know. - Not our main concern right now, mate.' Santa replied with a strained grunt as he fought off another gargoyle.

'Not our main concern?! Yes, it is. He's taking my sister.'

'I'm keen to help, but let's just save us for now,' Santa replied through gasps and thumping impacts of the fight. 'I'm pretty bad at saving lives when I'm dead.'

Aiden ducked as a spear flew past his head toward Santa and the massive-winged monster he was fighting, and he decided it best to keep his head down. Amazingly, Santa caught it and swung it quickly at his opponent's head, where it snapped in two, knocking the beast to the floor.

It was only now, as the two of them looked to where the spear came from, they noticed how thoroughly surrounded they were.

'Grab the reins,' Santa shouted at Aiden as he reached into a case in the back of the sleigh and pulled out a large crossbow and began shooting a spray of arrows all around them.

Very unsure of what he has doing, Aiden picked up the reins and looked at Santa in a panic. 'What do I do? How do I make it go faster?'

The big man in red continued to shoot at their enemies while dodging and deflecting spears and other attacks with his shield, further showing Aiden how underrated the legend of Santa was. 'Just pull the right-hand reign as hard as you can and yell 'hoo."

'Only the right one?' Aiden checked, a little confused.

'Yes, right now.' came the impatient yell back at him.

He pulled and yelled as instructed, which made him feel kind of silly, but Santa reached over his shoulder and gave it an extra tug when he saw Aiden wasn't as strong as the reindeer were used to. The sleigh took a very sharp and fast turn to the right, and they were now accelerating away from Sophie.

4

'Hey, turn this thing around.' Aiden yelled, attempting to pull the reins back the other way, but realised he had no chance.

'No mate, sorry, we have no hope if we keep going that way.'

'What? No, she has no hope without us. Where the hell are we going?' Aiden demanded angrily as he watched his sister getting further away. He turned toward Santa for his response, and noticed the fight was over, and the gargoyles had dropped right back.

'We're going to The Pole, so we can plan this rescue mission properly and bring the elves back with us. That way we will get your sister back, but if we go after them now, we all die. We can't do it on our own, I mean, we can't even get past his guards.' he added, pointing back at the gargoyles.

'The elves?' Aiden asked curiously.

'Yes, elves.'

'Elves are real?'

'Oh man, come on, of course they are. Dash, Dan, Rance,

Vick... The Elves!' Santa declared like Aiden should be completely familiar with their names, and when all he got was a look of confusion, he continued, 'Oh, come on, what is it with you people?'

'You people? What's that supposed to mean?'

'You people, you just don't get it. Dasher, Dancer, Comet, Vixen, these are not the names of reindeer. I'm Santa not Doctor Dolittle; I don't name reindeer. Those are the names of elves, my friends and family,' he explained as he watched Aiden's face change from confused to surprised, before ending up on excited.

'Oh, wow, and we're going to meet them?' Aiden asked.

'Yes, we must. I can't defeat this big ugly scum bag and his dopey friends on my own, so we call in the big guns,' he said with a chuckle, gesturing the size of a real elf, which is not big, but nowhere near as small as you would think either, and added, 'Also, they're cooking breakfast this morning, so yes, we really must.'

They continued to fly fast away from Krampus and his young prisoner. The good thing was, the gargoyles were not chasing them, and hadn't bothered following at all. They were there to stop unwanted visitors from following Krampus to The Black Rock, and that was all.

Aiden had a lot of questions bouncing around in his head, which would normally be fighting their way out of his mouth if his regular curious instinct was allowed to act. But this time he didn't speak any of them; he just sat there, staring up at the sky and thinking this strange night over in his mind.

He was trying to piece the night together in his mind and make some sense of it, but was coming up with nothing more than the insanity of the whole thing. He took a deep breath, ran his fingers through his hair and asked, 'What's The Pole?'.

'It's our home.' Santa replied.

'Alright, cool,' Aiden said, with his head slumping down looking at the floor, and continued, 'So we're going to your place to meet the elves, I get that, but why is it called The Pole?'

Santa roared with laughter.

'What?' snapped Aiden, annoyed at being laughed at.

'I'm sorry, but it's funny. You people named Santa's home the North Pole, not me. I just adopted The Pole for the name of our real home as a comedic homage to your fairy tale story of my life. It wasn't always called that.' he explained between laughter.

'I can't work out which parts of the Santa story are real, and which are made up,' Aiden said with a shrug. 'A few hours ago I thought the whole thing was made up.'

'Ah yes, The Legend of Santa. That does seem to have gotten out of control. Though we do get a lot of amusement out of parts of it.'

Aiden didn't really know what to think of this. He started the night with the idea of Santa stored in a part of his mind with unicorns, the tooth fairy and other mythical things. Then he saw the legendary man with his own eyes and he became real; a lot fitter looking than expected, but undoubtedly real, and with a sense of humour.

He shook his head and sat up straight. 'How much longer?' he asked.

'Another hour or so. But again, we're safe here, don't worry.'

'I'm not worried about us; I'm worried about my sister.' he said. Any brother in this position would be worried, and no amount of 'don't worry' was going to relieve that.

5

He leaned his shoulder on the side of the sleigh and looked down at the trees below. He couldn't see much, but he could smell plenty, and recognised the tickle in his nose as pine trees, which, his mind reminded him, meant Christmas trees.

After a short time of flying past the hills and valleys of pine trees, they were arriving. 'That's us down there, mate,' he heard Santa say, and he lifted his head up to see the big guy pointing up ahead, slightly to the left.

'You live in a forest of Christmas trees? I really don't know where the joke ends and the serious begins.'

'They're pine trees Aiden.' Santa said with a smirk.

'Yeah, Christmas trees.' he pushed back, and Santa just rolled his eyes.

He looked up a bit, still searching for what Santa had pointed to, and noticed some distant snowcapped mountains, and below them, a cluster of buildings.

'The Pole?' he asked, pointing at them.

Santa nodded his head and waved his arm with a flourish, like a game show model revealing a prize. Aiden looked out after the gesture, studying it as closely as he could, and was both surprised and impressed, though he didn't really know what he had expected.

Looking like a pile of log cabin-like buildings that had somehow spilled down the side of the mountain then neatly and thoughtfully stitched themselves together with beams, decks, and perfectly carved timber art, it was an impressive sight. Aiden thought the scene would look great on a calendar or postcard.

The whole place gave off a feeling of intentional and careful planning, which was obvious to anyone that knew elves; they had designed, built and put together every hinge, plank and bolt in the place. All the care in the world had been taken to ensure every little piece, no matter how small, was straight, clean, accurate and perfectly elvish.

Elves are very proud people, particularly when it comes to their work. It's fair to say they like to think a task inside out and plan every breath before lifting a tool. Given a week to complete a task, you could be sure of a good three days of it is used for planning, then another day for preparing meals, and it would still be done on time. As tradesmen, the work of an elf is genuinely flawless, and far beyond what you could expect from any human.

Paddocks had been divided up with little laneways so the horses could be separated from the reindeer, cows, alpacas, and other stranger creatures on the farm at different times. Open fronted sheds were stacked with hay, and silos filled with seeds and wheat. Crops were sown in the areas closer to the river for best access to water, and a large windmill turned with a slow yet powerful momentum to pump water up the hill to the gardens on the higher side of the main buildings.

These large, beautiful gardens grew the vegetables, fruits, herbs, and berries the seasons provided to the diet of the residents of The Pole.

As seasons changed, it was still cold enough to need a good jacket and a fire going, which the elves in this place seemed to have taken care of, with smoke rising from at least ten tall stone chimneys.

'So this is it?' Aiden said when he finished studying the place and received a wink and a nod of the head in reply.

He caught the first of the day's sun in the corner of an eye and turned to what he knew must be the east to see it rising above the distant hills, then turned straight back toward The Pole to look around in the improving light. As they got closer, he noticed there were people out working around the place, but they looked much more like regular people than elves. Some were gardening, others were cutting firewood, feeding animals, or other farm type chores; all of which he thought to be odd things for elves to be doing.

They swooped in and landed softly on the moist grass of a clearing between the edge of the trees and the complex of buildings, and as the reindeer slowly dragged them down on some well-worn tracks, it was clear they were home.

6

Aiden was in a far-away place within his mind, rolling Santa's words about Sophie's situation over and over, studying them and trying to find meaning where he wasn't sure there was any. All that mattered was they had to get to her quickly, and he was frustrated he seemed to be the only one with this level of urgency.

'Well, are you coming or not? Breakfast will be getting all cold and eaten.' Santa said excitedly, startling Aiden out of his deep thought.

They walked together down a long hallway to where Santa took his big red coat off and hung it on a thick nail on the wall. The hallway was lined with vertical timber boards up to waist height, with decorative wallpaper above it, and a carved picture rail where they met. The floor was aged yet perfectly maintained polished timber, with boards about a foot wide. He couldn't explain why, even to himself, but these features just felt to Aiden like the way Santa's place should feel.

It was only now, as he went to follow Santa's lead and also hang his coat up, he realised he wasn't wearing one, and embarrassingly was still in his pyjamas underneath his dressing gown. Santa noticed him looking down at himself and assured him there would be some new clothes for him inside. He thought about hanging up his dressing gown but decided to just keep it on.

They followed the hall around a corner to the left, then went up a short flight of stairs to a room where a long wooden table was loaded with food, and Aiden was excited to realise he was about to meet his first elves.

They were something else, not as he had expected. He looked around the room at these people and wondered who they were. Though he already knew other parts of the lore surrounding Santa had been very wrong, he just expected elves to be *elves*.

Well, they were elves, but just not the little ones he was prepared for. These were quite normal, and most of them surprisingly young looking people, regular people. Though in keeping a dash of truth back to the fairytale, they did have the little tweak of the ears that you have pictured in your mind.

Most of them looked busy. Some were bringing steaming plates of food to the table, one was cutting a strangely large loaf of sourdough bread, there was a young lady singing to herself as she made coffee, and others were cutting and pre-paring things Aiden couldn't quite identify.

He took in the beautiful range of smells and watched the incredible looking food continue to pile up on the table as he wondered how they could ever eat it all.

They stepped into the room and Aiden felt everyone turn

to look at him, but he tried his best to pretend he hadn't noticed, as he looked around the room, admiring its beauty. The lining boards from out in the hallway continued along the walls in here and wrapped right around the room, as did the wallpaper, which seemed to have changed in design, though it was impossible to pick the exact point of the change.

'Alright everyone, Elves, this is Aiden.' Santa announced, gesturing toward him with both hands like they should have been expecting him.

'Hey everyone.' Aiden reacted with one hand, waving around the room uncomfortably.

'Oh, and Aiden, this is…' and he started pointing around the room 'Dash, Dan, Rance, Vick, Comet, Coop, Donny, and I think I saw Blitz over the back there somewhere.' he finished, pointing toward the kitchen door. They all waved, and the close ones shook his hand as they all offered their own greetings.

'Go on. Eat, drink, and someone get this guy some clothes to change into.' Santa said, pushing Aiden gently towards the table and embarrassing him by reminding everyone he was in his pyjamas.

Santa pulled out a chair for Aiden, then one for himself to his right. 'The omelet is absolutely magic mate.' he said, winking at the female elf opposite them, who Aiden assumed had cooked it. He was right, the whole meal was fantastic, and made Aiden feel great. It was like he hadn't eaten for a week and had forgotten how good food could be.

Despite not being the cute little elves, he'd expected, Aiden found them to be a delightful bunch with plenty to like about them. There wasn't a common look about them that could be defined as what it was to be elvish. There was one elf in overalls, a couple in long black coats, a bright green tuxedo, an ill-fitted leather jacket, and one dressed in a pair of baggy rainbow trousers with what looked like a clear plastic vest. Some wore makeup, others, unnecessary glasses, strange hats or jewellery, and one of the long black coats was covered in little badges that looked like they came from some crazy old lady's garage sale.

'Did you manage to solve our little possum problem, Rance?' Santa asked one of the elves with a smirk.

'No, not solved,' she started as she loaded her bowl with some odd-looking bright pink fruit, then added 'But I did improve it.'

'How so?'

'Well, they're not eating our veggie garden anymore.' she said with a proud smile.

'Seems solved to me.'

'Yeah…' she started, and a few giggles started around the table. 'They've stopped eating the veggie garden, but only because I'm feeding them out the front.' she added, and the whole room burst into laughter at her idea to save the food by sacrificing food.

'Dash,' Santa started to speak to another of them through a mouth full of sausage when he stopped laughing enough to speak.

'Santa.' Dash replied with a cheeky grin over his coffee. He wasn't sitting back or relaxing. Instead, he seemed to be perched on the front edge of his seat, keen to hear the word to get into action. He looked to be the oldest of them by quite a bit but appeared to Aiden to make up for age in enthusiasm.

'You seen Dolph today?' Santa asked.

'No mate, why?'

Santa stuffed a piece of over-buttered bread into his mouth, then mumbled through it, 'We've got to make a trip up to The Black Rock,' which stopped all conversation around the table, switching every face to serious.

With this comment fueling thought, another elf chipped in. 'What's going on Santa?' This was Dan.

Dan sat a couple of seats away from Aiden towards the end of the table, but he hadn't taken much notice of him until now. Any time he'd looked in that direction his attention was snatched up by Blitz, who he had been watching him with nervous glances from the corner of an eye. He just looked like someone that should be glanced at with nerves; a wild-looking elf. He had a full sleeve of strange and distorted looking tattoos up one arm, a half buttoned up shirt, and a scar down most of his face that looked like it must have a violent story attached to it

Almost everything about Dan seemed to be in complete contrast to the vibe of Blitz, and he and Aiden would soon form a close friendship.

Santa took a deep breath and slid his plate away as a freshly poured coffee was passed to him and he told the solemn story of how Sophie found herself in need of rescue. There were many questions, and just as many comments, as Aiden noticed Santa silently communicating with both Dash and Dan through a series of glances and nods, before Dash got up and said he would go directly to speak to Dolph. Santa asked the others to arrange a lunch with the elvish wizard Dolph to plan the journey.

By the time Santa finished he had not only given the elves the details on what had got them into this situation, but he had also told Aiden about trolls and other concerns with fighting Krampus, including the mystery around The Black Rock itself, punctuated with regular comments about how good the food was.

Dan placed his knife and fork down on his plate and got

up. 'Come on, I'll get you some clothes then we'll show you a few things to keep you alive out there.' He said, hooking Aiden's interest with the last words, and led him out of the room down another long, thin hallway.

7

With breakfasts at The Pole often overlapping lunches, and the midday meal being planned with Dolph, Dan was keen to get Aiden through a bit of a self defence crash course first.

He showed him to the showers, set him up with everything he needed and left him to it. The clothes Aiden was given were very warm and comfortable, and the jacket had so many pockets there were even pockets with pockets, and it seemed to hug his body like it had been custom made. They even had a beautiful pair of soft leather boots for him.

'How's that feel?' Dan asked when Aiden walked out into the lounge room, newly washed and dressed.

'I feel great,' he replied. 'This outfit's amazing. Can I keep it?'

The only response he got to that was a laugh, which seemed to mean yes.

Dan turned to the counter in the corner of the room, then back to pass Aiden a coffee and a hot toasted ham and cheese sandwich.

Aiden raised a palm straight away to gesture no. 'More food? No. We just finished breakfast.'

'Yeah, one thing you'll probably notice is that elves love to eat. Don't mind a coffee either.' he replied, forcing Aiden to take one sandwich while he bit the other one himself as they walked out onto a balcony where two chairs and a cool breeze waited for them.

They sat quietly for a few minutes, sipping their drinks and eating their toasties, which Aiden had no interest in at all.

'What are you thinking?' Dan asked, noticing Aiden's thoughtful gaze into the distance.

'My sister. I'm thinking about Sophie. I'm worried about her.'

The elf sat for a moment and waited for Aiden to turn to look at him before responding. 'You heard Santa mate, we will get her back.'

'Yeah, that may be true, but she'd be scared, stuck out there with that thing, waiting to be rescued. - Wondering whether she will be rescued.'

'She won't have to wait long.'

'It's already been too long.'

'We can't just rush off unprepared, or we will fail, and fail hard. We need to plan the journey, and we need Dolph's help, which will happen very soon,' he looked down at his watch, then went on, 'And we need to make you into one of us if you're coming along.' Dan said.

'An elf?' Aiden looked at him, confused.

'No,' Dan answered with a laugh. 'We can't turn a human into an elf, I mean into part of the team, trained to survive and think like one of us.'

'Oh ok, and yes, I am coming,' he replied with certainty and added 'Tell me about The Black Rock. What's it like?'

'What do you want to know?'

'What's it like? I mean, what is it?'

'It's Krampus' place, basically. It's where he and his horrible kin live, it's where evil lives and grows, and it's where we want too not be. Once we get in there and find your sister, we'll be gone before they even know we've been there,' he replied, reluctant to continue discussing it, and moved to change the subject to start training. 'Alright let's get to it.'

'Lesson one: Trolls. These make up most of Krampus' army,' Dan announced in a different voice, like he had just switched to teacher mode. 'Big, thick and strong, and surprisingly quick for their size, but only in straight lines. And incredibly stupid.' Aiden smirked at the last comment, but realised from the look on Dan's face he was serious.

'I mean it mate, and I intentionally set out their strengths first, so you would see the need to take advantage of their weaknesses,' he said, pointing a finger at his own forehead. 'You're never going to out muscle one. I doubt even Santa could, but like I said, incredibly stupid - use that.' he repeated.

Aiden nodded that he was following along.

They moved into a dojo-like room, where Dan surprised Aiden with a display of troll weapons. He went through a tutorial of each one move by move, stepping Aiden through disarming, dodging, and out-manoeuvering to use the stupidity of the troll, along with their lack of agility, against them.

They thoroughly practiced a series of very simple strikes, followed by the well thought out series of counters, and repeated them over and over.

'Alright, I've got it,' Aiden said when he was getting bored and tired and feeling the pain of an unfit body being put through a real workout. Dan didn't stop, but instead moved from one move to the next faster, with increasingly explosive force. 'I'll tell you when you've got it. We stop when we're done, not when you're tired,' he said, continuing the training. 'They may be idiots, but if one of them hits you, you're dead. No injuries, just dead, one hit. Now keep going.'

When Dan was satisfied defending against and fighting trolls was understood, they took a seat as the lesson moved on to other aspects of troll behavior considered relevant to surviving them, and particularly avoiding them.

The conversation drifted off topic after a while as the two of them began to realise how well they were getting along, and after a good half hour of unproductive chat, Santa opened the door and entered the room with a carefully wrapped box in his hands.

He looked at the two of them on the couch and smiled as he crossed the room.

'How's progress?' he asked Dan.

'Better than expected, big man. He'll be ready in time. No problem,' Dan replied with an encouraging smile at Aiden.

'Well done, as usual,' Santa said to Dan as he stepped closer to Aiden with the box. It wasn't just a box; it was a long skinny flat box wrapped in green and red paper that featured detailed pictures, all finished off with a red bow on top – it was a present.

A present from Santa. A day earlier he had expected a present from Santa, but since then he had found the story of the delivery man Santa to be total rubbish, giving this gift real meaning.

'We want you to have this, Aiden,' he said as he handed the box over.

'Thank you"',' Aiden replied, nearly speechless, and he sat it down on the coffee table in front of him and started by removing the bow.

'So, what is it?' he asked.

'You do understand how the idea of a present works, don't you? You open it to find out what it is, I don't just tell you.'

It was only a small box. A few inches wide by slightly over a foot long, and quite flat. He picked it up and carefully examined it again, like he was trying to work out what it was before opening it, then put it back down on the table with a heavy thud and lifted the lid off.

His eyes opened wide with excitement as he saw it, like he wanted to expose as much eyeball as possible to this thing to take it all in. He reached into the box, picked it up and jumped to his feet, holding it out in front of him with pride.

'A sword!' he shouted with joy, really feeling like a kid on Christmas day. 'A little sword, but it's a sword. Is this really mine?' he exclaimed.

'Yes, it's yours, and it may look small now, but it will be exactly the size you need it to be, I assure you of that.' Santa explained.

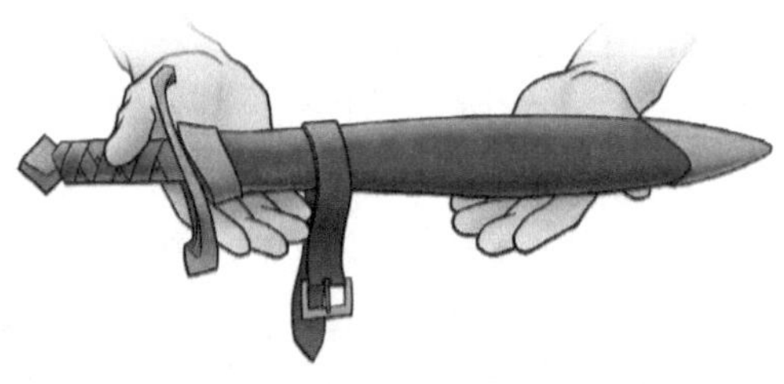

Aiden looked from Santa to Dan, slightly unsure what he meant. 'For what? Opening letters? Cutting up a roast turkey?' he joked with a grin, genuinely unsure what this dagger- like sword was for, though he certainly did like and appreciate it.

Santa laughed loudly. 'You're a funny boy Aiden. But seriously, Dan's going to give you some quick lessons on how to use a sword, and that,' he pointed at the sword. 'Will be your weapon.' Aiden raised a hand like a school kid with a question and began to speak, but Santa cut him off before he completed a word. 'Forget about the size of it. Learn to use it, and like I said, it will be exactly the size you need it to be.'

After a short chat with Dan about various items of farm maintenance and other work around The Pole, Santa said goodbye and left them to train.

8

They met for the lunch with Dolph in a different room. It was part room and part balcony. There were high ceilings (where there were ceilings at all) with a lot of exposed beams and rafters, which all seemed to be far thicker and deeper than they needed to be.

Main course didn't matter to Aiden. It was nice. He enjoyed it, but it wasn't nearly as memorable as the pudding. A large plum pudding was placed in the middle of the table and ceremoniously lit on fire before being served with cream and brandy butter. He was starting to think he might double in size if he stayed there too much longer.

When they finished the meal, including second dessert, Santa asked some of the elves to clear the dishes and set up so they could go over the map on the table, which they seemed to have been expecting, and went straight to it. He left them to get things ready and sat with Aiden out on the balcony. They looked out over the river and had a quiet chat.

'Why does Krampus do this?' Aiden asked from nowhere.

'Do what?'

'I don't know, all the evil. Why did he take my sister, and all those other kids before her?'

Santa thought for a moment, fidgeting as he examined the back of his hand and picked something out of a dirty and chipped fingernail, then spoke. 'You know how you like to be happy?'

'Yeah?'

'Why do you think that is?' he asked, confusing Aiden a bit.

'I don't know. It feels good.' he replied clumsily.

'Yeah. We all like to be happy, everyone does. That thing that happens to all of us; that great feeling making someone else happy brings us, he gets that from causing sadness. He's just backwards.'

It was a very strange explanation, but no one had ever been able to put it down to anything more, and it was fuel for Aiden's mind to burn as they sat there for a while more. Not a lot more was said, just some quiet small talk about the weather and Aiden describing a few things from home.

'Ready when you are big guy.' came an elf's voice from inside, now unmistakably serious.

'Thank you, Rance.' he replied to her kindly.

When they got back into the dining room, Aiden was surprised by the change. - The long straight edged table that was covered in the remains of lunch was gone and had been replaced by a round one with a large, detailed map laid out on it. Aiden sensed the smell of good food and merriment had even been replaced by serious business and dangerous conversation.

Gesturing at his side for Aiden to do the same, Santa took a seat at the table and looked over the map like it was an old friend he adored but was not pleased to see under these circumstances.

Aiden was beginning to feel comfortable there with the elves, and particularly with Dan and Santa, making him feel like part of the team, and part of a big and rather strange family.

Steaming pots of unusual smelling tea were placed around the table in the space between map edge and table edge. The festivity the wonderful meal had brought on was gone, with all faces now clearly switched from party to business.

There was Dan and Rance to Aiden's left, Santa on his right, Comet and Donny beyond him, then Dash, Blitz, Coop and Vick along the other side of the table, with another much older elf, who Aiden had not noticed before, in the remaining seat opposite him.

The older elf introduced himself as Rudolph, but the elves and Santa habitually called him Dolph. Aiden remembered this was the elf referred to as a great wizard; the one whose advice was so valuable on this. They made eye contact for a few seconds as Aiden thought about what they were doing and admired this cool-looking map, then looked up as Dolph looked across the table at him and winked with a tired grin.

The knowledge and skills of each individual elf around the table now began to show themselves to Aiden, and quite impressed him. They all contributed various facts, opinions and ideas, while Santa seemed to keep the conversation focused and on mission like he was chairing a board meeting, and for a long time Dolph just watched and listened as he compiled his own thoughts.

'Perfect, great idea.' one said, after Dash suggested the river would be still frozen at this time of year and could be used like a road they could drive the sleigh up straight to Krampus' front door, avoiding days of travel through the forest.

'Not a chance. It's melting. Have you seen the flows downstream?' Blitz objected.

'Yeah, water flows under ice.' came the argument.

'I say we just fly.' Donny declared boldly.

'And chance it with the gargoyles? No thanks.' came argument between the elves.

'No, gargoyles generally stay low. We can bypass them on a cloudy day.'

'Are we really going to risk it on 'generally'?'

'Have you ever seen one above the clouds?' came the response from Donny, not realising how naïve it sounded to everyone else.

'No, but...just no, this is not how we make decisions around here.' Dash argued.

Donny was still determined he was onto something. 'I'm telling you, if you want speed, the sky is the place to find it.'

Santa knew they needed stealth as much as speed, if not more, and could not afford to be seen or end up in a fight in the open sky on the way there. He moved to shut the argument down.

'Donny.' he said seriously, with a look that silenced the elf. Then before he had a chance to say any more, Dolph spoke.

'No one will be attempting a flight to The Black Rock,' and when the wizard spoke, they all froze in silence to heed every word. 'The idea of using the speed and surprise of a sleigh on the river is good, and it will be our chosen path. Once you make it through the section of forest to get onto the ice, you'll be there in no time.'

Donny dropped his argument, and all around the table accepted Dolph's words as final.

He then drew an old wooden wand from an inside pocket

of his long coat and began using it to point out landmarks, obstacles, and other items on the map. He pointed out that they would cross the river out the front of The Pole, where they would then travel over a couple of rather beautiful grassy hills and enter the forest, coming to the frozen upper section of the river from the southeast. He showed them the places they were most likely to come across trolls and jotted out their path on the map around these danger areas, leaving a trail of glowing light across the paper.

'He'll know we're coming, and though he's not too sharp himself, he knows elves are smart people. He will probably expect us to just take the most direct route there- the sky, because it's what he would do. But he also knows we will have other options, though he will have no idea what they are, so I expect trolls will be sent into the forest at random locations in the hope they might just stumble across us.' he explained seriously, and as he did so, he waved his wand above the map, summoning little trolls to pop up out of the paper and begin marching about aimlessly in groups.

'Even the most carefully designed route cannot plan around random wanderings of trolls.' Comet stated.

'Yes, correct Com, but what we can do is plan a route that sends us along the path least likely to be taken by trolls; meaning those most difficult for them to enter.'

'Alright, got it. They move in stupidly random ways, so we just avoid the obvious tracks the stupid would take?'

'Exactly.' Dolph agreed and continued to point out their path through to the entry point onto the frozen river, with the wandering mini trolls keeping mostly away from it and sticking to the easier and more obvious tracks as described by the old wizard as he went.

The path to rescue Sophie was now agreed, and it was time to prepare and get on their way.

9

Blitz and Coop went straight to collecting weapons and equipment, while Dash and Vick prepared the reindeer, and everyone else attended to other jobs that needed doing. There were reindeer and other animals to feed, blades to sharpen, bows to string, a sleigh to prepare, and all sorts of things around the place to make sure the rest of the elves would be able to run the farm while they were gone.

'How many times have you been up there?' Vick asked as she lifted a heavy saddle onto a reindeer and began clipping up and tightening straps.

'I don't know. A fair few.' Dash replied.

'Have you even seen it?' She responded doubtfully.

'What?'

'The Black Rock.'

'Yeah, I have, but there's seen it, and there's really seen it.' Dash replied, looking at Vick with a raised eyebrow.

'Go on.' Vick encouraged.

'Well, I know where it is.'

'That's not the same as having seen it.' Vick interrupted, and they went on with the packing.

They packed food, shelter and warmth for a few days, as well as a wide variety of weapons to fight off potential threats as they finished prepping the reindeer.

You've probably imagined a regular reindeer, or caribou, in your mind, and are thinking they would have the capacity to carry very little. This assumption is wrong and should serve as a warning about assuming anything as you continue through this story; some things here are just not the way you know them to be there. These reindeer weigh double that thing pictured in your mind, are all muscle, and made to work.

After feeding each of them and giving them a drink, the reindeer were checked for health and fitness. Once all was good to go here, saddles, bridles, and all strapping done up, the bags over the rear hips were attached next, followed by the big pack over the back end, with extra weapons strapped to the top.

10

It was raining when they left, but only lightly, and straight down; not that horrible sideways stuff you get in those storms where the wind makes you squint your eyes. It didn't last long; just enough to get everyone wet to start the day.

They took eight reindeer, with half of them pulling the sleigh and half being ridden by elves. If they are going to fly at all later down the track, they will need all eight pulling the sleigh to get it off the ground, but for now, just dragging it through smooth grass and mud along the ground, it is very light work for the four of them.

The route to the banks of the river was not so much long as it was difficult with its steep hills and winding tracks, but initially it was actually quite beautiful scenery if it wasn't for the dull, drizzling rain and the unfortunate reason that brought them there.

Aiden hadn't really been anywhere like this in his life. There were so many interesting things to see, things that he normally only saw on television. Even the river. It seems like a simple everyday kind of thing, but he had never been anywhere near a river like this before. He slowed down as they crossed the old stone bridge, which had been handmade by early elves many years ago, and he looked over the side to the rushing water below. It was like he could see the cold in the water, despite it being completely liquid and free from ice. Seeing the fish swimming below reminded him of the documentaries he used to watch with his dad on Sunday mornings of an old Englishman with a thick moustache fishing in some mystical looking land with little stone walls, bright green grass and shallow wide rivers.

'Come on mate, let's go. We can go fishing when we get back.' Donny said as he bumped into him, also not watching where he was going.

They went on following the path from the bridge toward the forest, with the stone paving continuing until the builders must have run out of stone and it slowly disappeared.

The hills to the left of the group were open and airy up to where they turned to forest further ahead. The grass that covered them was long and seemed to sway in the wind like it was waving to them.The parade of elves, with Santa leading the way on the big red sleigh up the front, followed the winding path off the stone and into a more sheltered section starting with a single lone willow tree, then another, then two more, and they were soon in an open alley way of greenery. They were giant trees. Aiden was familiar with willow trees. They weren't unusual around home, particularly along the path he would walk to school daily, and though he was sure that was what these trees were, he had never seen them even half this size.

The familiar smell of the willows eventually drifted away and was replaced by pine trees, along with another smell he couldn't quite identify, with a whiff of mud and moisture to it. They were moving from the open avenue of willows to the more dense and light blocking forest.

The rain had stopped, and with his nice new coat having kept him almost completely dry, other than his now only slightly damp hair, Aiden was bewildered by the feeling of moisture around him. The air was wet. Not in the way you feel when holidaying somewhere humid or tropical; but like a bucket of water was levitating around your head. The trees seemed to droop under its weight, with the pine needles pointing down, reaching to rest on the ground or whatever lay below.

'Man, it's getting cold in here.' he said to Dan, who was walking next to him, as a shiver surprised him as it ran through his body.

'Yeah, it's like its own separate climate in here, man,' Dan replied, crossing his arms tight across his chest and looking around at the trees above them. 'Give it a minute. We'll pass through it and hit a warmer section up here.'

The path peaked to a bit of a crest, and an eerie whirring sound washed through Aiden's head as the pine needles high above them rubbed together with the breeze. It continued for such a time that it left him wondering whether it was still going, or just trapped inside his head, echoing around in there.

They went up and down hills, then up again and up some more before going down a bit, which after repeating for a few hours left most of the group clueless whether they were up high or down low. The dense forest only allowed vision for a short distance all around which, combined with the thick ceiling of leaves and branches above, was quite disorientating.

Time was another thing hard to keep track of in there. With no chance of seeing the sun's position in the sky, and such a boring walk that seemed to be just more of the same looking trees and rocks over and over, time seemed to be dragging out forever. With the feeling of hunger in their stomachs and the demands for a rest coming from a few tired elves, a reason to stop would be welcomed by all.

A trickling sound up ahead got the attention of a few of the group. Some had it pointed out to them, as they were surprised by a family of rabbits having a drink, who looked up at the approaching group and promptly took off. Though it was full of other greenery and life, there wasn't a lot of grass in the forest, and as well as a source of water, the rabbits had known this little stream to be one of the rare places lined with food. It was quite a pretty site, really; a perfectly clear stream of water, through which an interesting variety of small stones could be seen sparkling on the bottom. Both sides of the waterway were lined with grassed areas a good few metres wide and continued from a thicker area of ferns further up the hill, to where the water took a dive into a rock pool down the hill a little way. The green ground-covering seemed to have been contagious, with the bases of the old trees and giant rocks in the surrounding area also partly covered by a mossy slime, like it was climbing over them.'Let's take a quick break here. If the water's good for rabbits, it's good enough for us.' Santa announced, pointing downstream to where the rabbits had gone.

The elves got down from the reindeer and out of the sleigh and made their way down onto the soft grass area to take up a spot to rest their legs, with some even laying down for a moment. Santa climbed up onto a big old moss-covered stump to see what he could see up ahead, and a few of the more tactically minded elves took Dash's lead and had a good look around before allowing themselves to relax, then moved in around Santa to hear any thoughts that were coming.

11

From where he stood up on his round green platform, he was able to look right out over the top of the low shrubs and ferns, past where the creek took a dive over a chunk carved out of the hillside, and into the valley below.

'Something has been through here.' Santa said quietly.

Dash issued some fast and quiet instructions, and Dan and Coop responded with stealth, climbing onto a couple of branches that provided the right view, and each drew an arrow to their bows and scanned for a threat.

'All good, guys,' Santa responded to their instincts. 'Down in the valley ahead. Someone's been through recently, but they're gone.'

'Krampus?' Aiden asked, somewhat hopefully, having overheard the observation.'No mate, we won't see him around here.' Santa explained.

'What then?'

'Something big. Probably trolls, and looking at the tracks

they've left, like a herd of mammoths have been through, there must have been quite a few,'"' he said, then looked around to the rest of the group, 'Come on, do what you've got to do, and let's get down there for a look,' he said, then added as he jumped down from the stump, 'And let's keep it quiet, I don't know how close they might be.'

As most of the group took a moment for a drink, grab a piece of fruit from the back of the sleigh, or adjust straps on their reindeer, Santa waved Dan and Coop down from their perches and sat with them on the end of a big log for a moment as he also called Dash over. 'What do you think?' he asked, looking at Dash, who he expected to have some wise advice on the subject.'I really want to be sure it was trolls that did that before going down there.' Dash said, looking down the hill thoughtfully.

'What else could it have been?' Coop asked.

'I don't know mate; it could have been anything. I mean yes, it does clearly look like something big came through, but it could have been a few moose, or even just a big pack of something smaller; I've seen packs of wolves do that kind of damage.' Dash explained.

'That's not what you're concerned about though.' Dan suggested.

'No. There are plenty of other things in this place for us to be worried about, and they're not all as stupid as trolls.'

'Like what?' Coop asked.

'It doesn't matter what; we don't even know about some of the monsters that live through these parts, and some of them may be smart, and could be watching us at any time.' Santa stated, prompting them all to look around nervously.

'Ok,' Dash started and took a deep breath as he looked around at them all. 'Option one; those tracks and broken trees down there were caused by trolls. If we're careful and quiet, we will sneak in behind them and control that battle enough to win it. Not a problem. Option two; it was a big pack of something less sinister, animals, whatever, no problem.'

'What are you suggesting? We have to go down there, there's no other way for us to get through.' Santa said.

Dash looked over Santa's shoulder toward the other side of the creek and the ridge that roughly followed parallel to the valley below, and its trail of broken branches and crushed shrubs. 'Yes, there's no other way for the sleigh, but there's another way on foot,' he said pointing to the alternative path, and they all nodded along, beginning to get where he was going with it, as he continued, 'You lot continue on down the path and through the valley, quietly and carefully, and I'll stalk across the ridge with these two and cover you from where we can see what's going on. If it's an ambush, we'll know before it happens.' he finished, emphasising the 'quietly and carefully'.

By the time they finished talking, everyone else was ready to move off and were waiting impatiently. 'Come on, there'll be plenty of time to chat later, you lot.' Blitz called from the front of the sleigh.

Santa said goodbye to Dash, Dan and Coop, then stepped up into the sleigh to take his place beside Blitz. 'Be safe.' he said to the elves left standing at the green rest site as he and the rest of the group started down the hill toward the suspicious tracks.

'Will do big guy. We'll stay hidden, but if we see anything bad up ahead, we'll stick an arrow between your feet as a signal to stop.' Dash replied in a tone that sought approval.

'Yeah, good man. We'll keep an eye out.' Santa confirmed, assuming and hoping he wasn't literally meaning the signal arrow would be put between his feet.

'We better get ahead of them.' Dash said as the three

of them started walking toward a place to jump across the little waterway. He wasn't saying anything they didn't already know. These three were a good team that had worked together a lot over the years, who got along and cooperated very well. They hopped across a fallen tree, then onto a flat rock ledge on the other side and took off in a steady jog up the hill, cutting the corner toward where the sleigh would soon be following the rampaged path in the valley. Dan ran at the front, followed by Dash, then Coop at the back.

They picked up the pace a bit and trotted through the moist rain forest, where they saw more of the same slimy, moss-covered wood, and incredible fungi became more numerous as they went. The moss was slippery, and they had to be careful to avoid crunching sticks and leaves on the forest floor as they tried to get through the area quietly, and get to the next crest to be in the best position before Santa and the crew hit the path below.

'Want me to go high?' Coop asked as they took off again.

Dan and Dash looked at each other for a second, communicated silently with their eyes, then agreed with a nod. Dash responded, 'Thanks Coop, it's your playground up there, mate.'

He ran with them for a few more steps, then diverged from their path onto a nice straight log conveniently ramped up. He sprinted up it, leaping from the end and grabbing onto a thin branch with both hands. His legs swung back and forth as he built the momentum needed, then threw himself to the next limb in front of him, which was slightly higher, and landed perfectly on both feet.

Finding his footing, he looked down to Dash and Dan who were still running at a steady but quiet jog while keeping an eye on him and gave them a thumbs up. They returned the signal. Once up there, the agility and skill of this young elf was really quite impressive. He skipped and jumped from one branch to another, kicked off trunks, and ran from tree to tree across the flimsiest of branches simply by knowing and trusting he wouldn't be staying on the thinner limbs long enough to break them. There was a slight shake of the trees as he moved across the canopy from one to the next, which once he got going was far faster than the elves on the ground below, but he knew they were a team, and each played an important role.

Perched high in a tree almost directly above where the sleigh would soon be passing, Coop made a discrete bird-like whistle to get the attention of the other two on the hill. Dan and Dash had now each taken up a suitable spot to monitor the area, about two hundred meters apart. Dan heard and recognised the whistle and returned another similar whistle of his own. Then Dash followed, as they used their own little code to tell each other where they were and what they were seeing.

Santa steered the sleigh down the steep incline and around a couple of almost impossibly tight corners. Then the reindeer were able to get some better space to move in and dragged the sleigh onto the already damaged track.

'What are you thinking big guy?' Blitz asked quietly as they turned into the trail of destruction, really doing his best to take advantage of this front seat, and take the lead alongside Santa.

'I don't know Blitz. I'm not sure, but I'm becoming more certain that this is the clumsy work of a group of trolls.' he replied thoughtfully, as he looked around, examining anything he thought might contain information.

'I was thinking the same thing,' Blitz agreed, then added, 'The further we go the more uncomfortable I am with this whole thing.'

'What do you mean?' Santa questioned.

'I don't know, I just don't like it. This whole rescue expedition just seems off to me. I mean, why did he take her? Why is he back?'

Santa thought for a few quiet minutes and sighed. 'I know Blitz, something is definitely off, but it doesn't really matter, we have to do it.'

'Yeah, I know, and I agree, but that doesn't mean I like it. We're walking into something more, and we all know it, but are for some reason pretending we don't.'

They continued on for a few more minutes in near silence, with only the sound of light steps of the slow-walking reindeer hooves and the scrape of the sleigh runners through the dirt. Then Santa's senses confirmed the suspicion in his mind. 'If that smell's not troll, I'm the Easter bunny,'''' he said sniffing sharply as he looked around, then turned to Blitz, 'Load the crossbow.'

Blitz got up and turned to the elves behind him in the next row of seats, who had also understood the request and handed over the equipment. Blitz took the oversized black crossbow in both hands and heaved it over Santa's head as he ducked to avoid wearing it, then dropped the pivot pin into the hole in the front of the sleigh with a heavy thud. Thick steel arrows with broad pointed heads were then passed over and clicked into a specially prepared mounting bracket. Blitz took one and loaded it into the weapon, then cranked it back ready to fire. This was a move not taken lightly, and the elves all knew if Santa had called for the sleigh nose to be armed, they should also prepare themselves for whatever he was suspecting may be about to happen.

The elves were now hesitant and on edge as they went, senses were in a heightened state. They all jumped when they passed underneath Coop, sitting watching over them quietly, as he dropped a small pebble into Santa's lap. The big-bearded man was so on edge already he jumped back with fright so hard it caused everyone else on board the sleigh to do the same, then seconds later they looked up to see the well-hidden elf in the tree waving at them to let them know where he was.

They went on for quite a while from here without an event of any kind, as the elves on the hills and in the tree kept an eye on things from above. Then they noticed something unusual. It wasn't something concerning or worrying; and it's difficult to even explain how it was noticed. It only seemed like something you would raise an eyebrow and look closer at, but not worry too much about. Something about the forest had changed. It just felt different, like the trees were somehow conspiring to do something not yet clear.

The elves and Santa exchanged nervous glances and gestures across the sleigh, as Aiden too began to feel the change.

'What's wrong?' he asked Santa, who ignored the question and instructed everyone to keep moving.

12

As they rode on for the next few minutes, they all began to feel as though the forest was closing in around them.

'Anyone else feeling claustrophobic on this track?' Aiden asked no one in particular.

'Yeah, it's a thick patch of forest.' Rance dismissed from on a reindeer up front, though she didn't even believe what she was saying.

They continued for a few hundred metres more, becoming darker and more closed in as they went, communicating only through silent gestures and subtle movements of eyes.

'No, this is something else,' Santa broke the silence. 'Get us out of here, I don't like the feel of this.' He pointed to two of the elves on reindeer back, then the other two. 'Two up front and two drop back.' he ordered.

Rance and Vick both drew swords and moved in front of the group and the other two dropped off to guard their back, and they all increased their speed.

Almost like they were reacting to the acceleration, the trees began to move faster, changing from being so smooth and discrete it was hard to pick exactly what was happening, to being so obvious, and even quite confronting as they moved.The trees were not only growing out of the ground now at a rate of a few feet per second, they were also sprouting horizontal branches, reaching out to one another to create a wall.

Santa recognised even though this wall of trees moved fast and looked strong, it was not attempting to block their way at all. There were both good and bad points to the situation being assessed in Santa's mind. The good was they were free to continue along the path as they wanted to, but the bad was they could no longer leave the path even if they wanted to, giving the feeling they were being funnelled into something.

He asked Aiden to move to the next row of seats and sit in the middle directly behind him, then turned and nodded to Blitz, who was the only other one left in the sleigh with them and knew exactly what Santa was communicating. He moved back and stood beside Aiden, drew an arrow, and stood ready with his bow raised and arms taut as Santa took a tight grip on the big crossbow mounted on the front.

'I hope there's some tension on your bows back there, elves, I'm getting a strong smell of troll scum up here.' Rance said flatly.

'Can you guys see this from down there?' Coop called to the two on the ground below, deciding the time for quiet may have passed.

'Yes, but I'm not sure what it is I'm seeing. What's happening?' Dan asked back, hoping the higher viewing point allowed Coop to make sense of it.

'I don't know, it looks like something's folding the trees

over on themselves, collapsing them onto the path. Dash?' he described as he walked out along a wobbly thin branch and hopped from it to another on the next tree, hoping, as usual, Dash would be able to further enlighten them.

'Can you see what's doing it?' Dash replied.

'No, it's hard to see much at all. Should we get closer for a look?' came Coop from above, where he was continuing to slowly move from tree to tree above their friends on the changing path below.

'Forget sneaking, we're no use to them up here. We need to get to them fast. They're in trouble, go, go!' Dash declared, making it clear in his mind this situation had escalated from monitoring from a distance to racing to save lives, yelling loudly by the time he finished, as the trees closed in around their friends.

'Rance, Vick, drop back.' Santa ordered in a clear voice, breaking from the whispers they had been using, as he had a change of strategy.

'You taking the lead?' Rance asked.

'Yeah, whatever this is we're being led into; we're going at it hard,' he said as he stood up like a gladiator in a charging chariot at an ancient colosseum, adjusted the big crossbow to be shooting down the middle between the reindeer, and yelled a cry of 'Hooo!' as he gave the reins a sharp snap with his free hand, and they accelerated into whatever waited for them up ahead.

The sound of the reindeers' hooves beating a hard and fast tune on the cool damp path echoed through the timber tunnel that surrounded them, combining with the creaking of the trees rubbing against each other as they bent and twisted around them, creating quite a noise. They charged on into the unknown through several bends and up and down rises and dips, as Coop sprinted through the trees above

them, jumping from branch to branch, swinging on giant handfuls of leaves and pine needles to gain as much momentum as he could to throw himself forward and get in front of the forest closing in around the sleigh. Dan and Dash were left somewhere in the back of his mind as he focused on catching up to see what it was doing this.

As the path took a sharp turn to the right, and conveniently toward Coop, he was able to get his first look at the sprint they were now in, and the fully armed sleigh being driven at maximum speed by a raving Santa who stood ready with mounted crossbow.

At the end of the still developing timber tunnel, Coop saw a group of trolls standing waiting with weapons ready and what looked from high in the trees like a couple of wolves chained by their side, ready to attack. The sleigh was getting close now; Coop guessed maybe a couple of hundred metres away; two bends. He ran faster, jumped, ran, and jumped again, pulled an arrow from the quiver at his right shoulder and released it toward a space in the bending trees slightly ahead of his friends.

'Thwack.' Santa looked down at the arrow lodged in the floor of the sleigh at his feet and yelled clearly and loudly, 'Coming up on them now, elves. He we go,' recognizing the message this arrow had delivered, in this rather amazing shot that very few of them could have made.

Coming around the last corner and over a slight rise, Santa only needed to see the first set of eyes looking back at him and he let the first of his heavy black arrows fly, spinning through the air between the reindeer, and taking out the first troll as the sleigh burst into the clearing right into the group. The pack of monsters split down the middle as they ran to get out of the way of the charging reindeer, with one of the wolves getting kicked and head-butted over, before they came to a stop then turned to face the enemy.

Arrows flew and swords clashed as the trolls tried to take on this team of elves and their powerful leader in the big dirty red coat, and though there were plenty of injuries, and some sore elves to come out of this, Santa quickly overpowered the last of them, and the evil gang Krampus had sent out there was defeated.

Wounded, exhausted and victorious, they all collapsed to the ground in relief. 'Everyone alright?' Santa asked, and received answers from all, some more pained than others, and a few reporting more injuries than most.

'You alright kid?' he asked Aiden, who was still up in the sleigh. 'Yeah, I'm fine. That was insane. Are you ok?' he asked back, looking at Santa's bruised face and scratched hands.

'All good, just a few knocks and bruises, nothing to worry about.' he said, wiping his face onto the dirty sleeve of his coat and picking up his sword as he got up.

The elves were working their way around, picking each other up, checking on each other and slowly coming together. They all gathered around Rance and Donny, who had taken the most damage, with some quite severe injuries that needed first aid before they went much further.

'I'm going to have to patch these ones up before we move Santa,' Dash said, 'Can you bring the sleigh over here a bit, and someone get my first aid bag out of the back.'

A few neat stitches, a firm bandage and a bit of medicine, and they were all up and about with nothing more than a slight limp and an arm in a sling.

13

Having been funnelled through a crazy tunnel of timber and leaves before chaos overcame them, they now left the fight scene in the only direction that was available to them, and when they finally found a place that seemed safe to stop a couple of hours later, none of them had even the most uneducated guess at which way they should be going next. Not a clue. It wasn't that one elf thought they should go one way and another claimed the opposite. No, none of them had any idea.

What they did know was they needed a good feed and somewhere to rest for the night, so those who came out of the fight in the best health, strung a bit of a canvas between a couple of trees for some shelter, started a fire, and planted a few trip lines around the place to alert them of any more unwanted visitors that may have been around.

Aiden didn't feel great about what had just happened, specifically the role he played in it – none. He kept the newly

gifted sword in the leather sheath strapped to his left forearm, with the hilt at his wrist and the point extending just past his elbow. This was an unusual way to carry a sword, and though it only works for a weapon up to a limited small size, Dan repeated the fact that it would be more useful this way. As he fitted the custom-made leather pouch to Aiden's arm the day he was given the weapon by Santa, he explained. 'It doubles as a sort of piece of armour for the forearm, and it is always *right there.*'

But with all the excitement of the new weapon in its specially designed custom sheath, and the magical potential, he regretted not using it when they were ambushed by the trolls. He regretted not doing more than holding it up like he was presenting it to them at Show and Tell.

'Just remember your training and go over it in your head when you don't need it; as we walk, when you sleep, whenever. We all freeze up the first time. You'll be fine.' Dan assured him.

Aiden was just as confused as everyone else in relation to where they were and where they were going, or probably even more, but he was a real thinker, and he began turning over possibilities in his mind. He asked himself the simple question of what a person needs when lost to find their way, and the very obvious answer of a map came to him.

'There's a map.' he said loudly and unexpectedly.

'What?' Blitz snapped back annoyed, assuming this kid had nothing useful to contribute in a situation like this.

He got up and walked over to the back of the sleigh to an old red bag lying sideways, half open, where he had seen Rudolph deposit the big round map from the meeting table.

'No. Oh, no.' the elves heard him say to himself.

'No, no, no, no, no!' he repeated louder and louder, with his hands on his head as he dropped it on the seat.

Santa stood up and walked towards him, concerned 'What is it? What's wrong?'

Aiden picked up the destroyed map in a big ball in his arms and pulled off individual pieces, holding them up to Santa. 'We can't read this. We'll never find Sophie now.' It looked like it had been through a paper shredder.

'Let me see. These elves can fix anything.' Santa said with open arms to take the map.

Aiden knew it couldn't be fixed, he felt like he was losing his sister as he realised this, and he took it out on Santa, throwing the ball of ruined map hard into his chest, then stomping off to sit alone.

Rance and Dan took the bundle from Santa, with no chance of Rance letting a slight injury keep her out of this. That's all it was, a dirty old bundle of torn paper that hardly resembled a map at all anymore, but they cared about Aiden and the mission they were on, so they took it over by the fire to inspect it in the light and see what they could do with it.

'Let us work our elvish magic on it mate.' Dan told Aiden, in an effort to give the kid some hope, and Rance added 'How dare you doubt us.' with a cheeky grin.

They laid out a big square canvas sheet that was usually their tent in wetter times and gave themselves a nice clean and flat surface to work on. Dumped in the middle of the canvas, the so-called map just looked like a pile of half mulched leaves from the forest floor.

They considered themselves to be very capable at even the most difficult of jig-saw puzzles, which was a common evening activity at The Pole, but this one was far beyond them. They couldn't even work out which way was up for most pieces. Just mess on the top and mess on the bottom.

'Dude, what the hell is this stuff, anyway?' Dan asked, holding up one of the larger pieces toward Santa.

'That side looks like mud, and I think that splatter might be troll blood, but I have no idea what the rest is, or how it got so badly damaged.' the big man replied.

'I was just wondering the same thing. It's very strange.' Dash added as he walked around the fire to stand beside the mess to get a better look. He stood with his hands on his hips, examining it, and continued. 'Obviously the trolls don't want us to ever get to The Black Rock, which may even be why they were here – that was no chance encounter, but to target our map seems a long way above the intelligence of any troll.'

Santa walked closer and stood with Aiden and Coop, whose attention was taken by Dash's words. 'You make a very good point Dash; I didn't know trolls were that smart.'

'It doesn't matter how it happened. Can you put it back together or not?' Aiden snapped at Dan and Rance, who he considered to be his friends, but he was unfortunately now taking out his frustration and fear on them.

No one spoke for a while. They all just looked down at the pile of paper before them, glancing at each other quietly, thinking the same thing. Dan stood up. 'I'm sorry mate, this would take us days; days we haven't got. Let's get some sleep and we'll push on in the morning without it. We'll find our way somehow.'

They locked eyes for a long moment until Aiden felt tears building up and he lunged forward to the pile of rubbished map. Dan and Rance didn't know what he was doing and just got out of the way as he bent down and pushed it all into a heap. He got on his knees and wrapped his arms around the dirty torn pile and picked it up, twisted toward the fire, and threw it all in the air.

The pieces flew from his arms and out over the whole fire, each piece drifting down slowly like autumn leaves to the forest floor and settled over it, looking ironically like one flat sheet. At first it seemed to be smothering the fire, then the pieces began to glow, and became brighter and brighter to the point they were expected by all to burst into flames, but they did not.

Instead, a thick smoke of many shades of grey rose from the pieces as they smouldered like wet wood that refused to burn but insists on smoking the place out. The smoke built up and blew about in a little cloud that seemed to be getting pumped into one spot right on the fire, like some weird mis-firing smoke machine, then all at once the dark grey cloud began to rise, and strangely just stopped and hovered a few feet from the ground.

Everyone stared at it, with no idea what was happening. None of them had ever seen smoke behave like this before. It was just hanging there in the air, not rising into the sky, and some of the elves started to get to their feet for a better look. 'Aiden, you're a genius.' Santa mumbled as he watched the smoke, fascinated.

'I am?'

'Yeah, you are,' Santa replied, confusing him. 'I didn't know what you were doing. I thought I was seeing a childish tantrum, but I now see I've underestimated you.'

'What're you talking about?' came the voice of an elf in the dark.

'What's going on?' added another.

Still watching the smoke mix about in a now flattening cloud before them, Santa explained. 'When we were packing the sleigh, Dolph folded up the map and put it in my bag in the back, and as he did so he was reassuring Aiden the map was there to guide us, and it was one hundred percent reli-able. The last thing I heard him say to the kid was 'The map's not on the paper, it's in the paper. If it catches fire, I hope you all can read the smoke.' I didn't know what he meant at the time, and didn't think much of it, but it couldn't be clearer now.' he finished with a grin, as they all watched the smoke form the shapes of trees and mountains. It moved and swirled and bubbled about as if trying and struggling to get it right, before it settled itself as a perfect copy of the land they were coming from, going to, and all in between and beyond.

The detail was incredible, perfect, and everyone moved in close in a circle to admire it with fascinated eyes.

'Alright, this is awesome, even for Dolph.' Donny said with a grin.

The new map of smoke showed not only The Pole, but it also showed little creatures moving around which, though they looked more like ants at this size, were their livestock, and even a few elves.

'Is this a live map of real stuff?' Blitz asked as he watched the grazing ants.

As well as The Pole, The Black Rock also captured their attention, with more than a few elves trying to get a closer look to see which of the stories were true, and what it was actually like, though this area was misty and unclear. Linking the start and the finish of this great journey was the route as it had been marked as a trail of light from Dolph's wand on the round table back at The Pole.

Following this line, what quickly became clear was the chaos of the last few hours had seen them diverge from the planned route.

'Hey that's us.' Blitz said excitedly, pointing at the little smoky figures standing around a floating map.

'And the little smoke you just pointed at the map. Unbelievable Rudolph.' Donny added, laughing in disbelief.

'Alright, we've got to get back on course,' Santa said, switching to leader mode and automatically thinking strategy.

'There seems to be a high amount of activity right through-out the forest, but I can't tell who or what most of it is. If we can just get back on course, the river isn't far away,' he said, pointing back and forth between themselves and the river. 'If we just continue through this valley, we'll come to that creek we stopped at back up the hill there, and if we follow that, it will lead us all the way to the river.' he continued, pointing as he spoke.

'We follow a creek of liquid water into a frozen river?' Donny asked, unsure of whether he understood correctly or he was asking a stupid question.

Santa giggled as he started, 'Yes, very good Donny, good point, we have to come onto the river further upstream, above the rocky falls, where it's still frozen,' he explained, pointing to an area just short of the river as he spoke. 'We'll have to cut across somewhere here.'

'Yeah, it almost never freezes below the falls.' Dash added.

'These packs of animals or trolls, or whatever they are,' Dash started, pointing at some figures amongst the trees of smoke. 'I'm concerned that if we cross paths with them, there could be all sorts of trouble for us, and the risk of another big delay or detour. And I'm assuming this map thing only works once.'

'So what are you suggesting?' Santa asked, hoping Dash was presenting a solution, not just a problem.

'I'm suggesting that we leave soon so we can at least get a head-start on this while it's still dark. Once we hit that river, we avoid all of them,' he explained, pointing to everything upstream of where they enter the river, then continued, 'And from there it's a very fast ride to Aiden's sister, but most importantly we first need to get to that river.'

A lot of elves nodded their heads and discussed it in

mumbles and mutters between themselves. Then silence settled to allow Santa to be heard.

'You each know how you feel and what you need to do for yourself, so get some rest, eat, fix any weapons, or do whatever you need to. We leave in an hour.' The group dispersed to attend to various tasks, leaving Aiden and Dash standing with Santa to examine the map further.

14

They travelled with caution for the first few hours through the early morning darkness and through the first of the day's sunlight. They were all a bit bruised from the attack. They had lost a little layer of the confidence they usually had in their team's ability to spot this kind of attack and flip it to their advantage.

'Ready to kick the pace along a bit?' Santa said to Dash after a while.

'Yeah mate, we're good to go, we've just been hanging back to give everyone a rest.'

'We're alright, lets push on. It's no good getting there all rested and healed if it's too late for Sophie.' he spoke.

'Aiden been in your ear?' Dash assumed, with a bit of a grin.

'Yeah, he's keen, and fair enough too.' he confirmed, giving Dash a look he knew meant he was serious.

'Do you think we'll hit the ice by the end of the day?' Aiden asked Santa, feeling encouraged by their better pace.

'On the river?'

'Yeah? Will we get there today?'

He thought for a moment as he watched Aiden flipping his little sword about in his hands, becoming more comfortable and familiar with it, and replied, 'Yeah, if we're not on the river by dark, we'll be very close.'

By mid-afternoon; much earlier than most of them had expected, they were nearing the river. Coming around a sweeping bend in the path, they saw it. Santa stopped them for one final break, and they strapped all the reindeer to the sleigh harness, ready to hit the ice.

Santa took the reins again now, with Dan and Dash on each side of him, talking him through the approach to the river, with emphasis on the need to hit it hard and accelerate right away. They didn't know what they might come across when they hit the ice, as they were going to be completely exposed, so any elves good with a bow were ready to attack.

Squashed in behind Santa, between Blitz and Donny, though it seemed like they still had significant distance to go, Aiden felt so close to his little sister; like there was real hope. The frozen river would provide a clear and direct route right to The Black Rock, he remembered the explanation, and as Santa had later reiterated in the smoke map, they would be able to go so fast once they hit the ice that nothing would catch them. At that kind of speed, he was sure it wouldn't take long before they arrived and he held his sister in the tight hug he had thought of constantly since the night he stood in his front yard and watched her disappear.

15

They turned that last wide sweeping corner and saw the river through the trees, with the low sun now reflecting sharply off its surface. 'Alright big guy, let's go.' Dash started, pointing at a bunch of small ferns up ahead where the track turned away to the right. 'We want to leave the track and break straight through there onto the riverbank, and down onto the ice.'

Santa took the advice and snapped the reins up and down, barking orders to the reindeer to speed up, and felt himself tense up at the uncertainty ahead as they began to accelerate and bump about.

A spray of ice shavings covered the front of the sleigh as they hit the frozen surface of the river, almost losing control. 'Turnnnn!' Dash yelled as he pulled Santa's hands as hard as he could to the left.

The momentum that drove them through the shrubs and onto the ice was pushing them straight ahead towards the other side of the river. They were turning hard, and the reindeer responded, pulling upstream to the left as hard as they could, but they were slipping, drifting sideways towards the riverbank, where they now saw there were trolls waiting.

'Hoooo!' Santa continued waving the leather straps about frantically in desperate attempts to get them moving in the right direction. He glanced back and forth to the trolls getting closer on his right. There must have been at least ten or fifteen of them, but no one had a moment to consider counting them. A couple of them wore armour, and one had an old metal helmet on that looked strangely far too small for its head, but in general they appeared to be unprepared for a fight.

The first troll to see the out-of-control sleigh overflowing with passengers sliding toward them, ran out of the trees with a kettle in its hand and stopped at the river's edge. He turned and yelled something strange back at his friends, who were only partly visible on the edge of the forest, paused to listen for a response, then threw the kettle at the sleigh with a roar, before turning to walk away. The old iron kettle flew right over them and slid along the ice toward the other side of the river.

Aiden watched it pass overhead, stood up and looked toward the troll, and yelled, 'A kettle? You'll need more than kitchen appliances to stop us.' as they continued to drift slowly toward the riverbank.

'Sit down and shut up.' Blitz snapped, shoving him back down into his seat firmly, ensuring to scare any idea of doing that again right out of him.

Though their sideways

movement was slowing, with the reindeer stomping away at the ice trying to force them upstream, the kettle throwing troll was now picking up a rock, which looked much more dangerous than the kettle. It was a dark grey rock about the size of his head, which he picked up in one hand and pulled his arm back like a baseball pitcher ready to launch a fast ball.

'Shoot him Blitz!' Santa yelled urgently as he saw the pitcher stepping up to the edge of the ice and shifting its weight, readying itself to put its vast mass into the throw.

Blitz said nothing and immediately fired the arrow he already had loaded in his bow and sunk it straight into the troll's tough, fatty torso.

As it hit the ground and the rest of the trolls on the bank turned to look out onto the river, they roared back through the trees and began throwing anything available at the sleigh. 'Ho, ho, ho.' Santa barked at the reindeer as spears, steel tools, and all other means of dangerous objects flew at them, with a few even hitting the side of the sleigh. They were now beginning to move in the right direction, with the thunder of hooves on the ice finally having an impact, as a shower of arrows from the rest of the elves put a stop to the trolls' attack as they sped away.

'Alright everyone, keep low and hang on tight. We're really going to get moving now.' Dash said over his shoulder as Santa urged the reindeer to speed up.

The river wasn't perfectly straight, but the bends were gradual and able to be negotiated at high speed, so they took each one fast than the last, as their speed continued to increase. Santa continued to crack the reins at them and yell instructions, which changed when Dash suggested he begin speaking to them as if they were in the sky, not on a river.

'Get up 'em Santa, tell them to fly.' he supplied.

'You know we can't possibly fly with this many of us in here.' Santa argued.

'Of course, I know that. I didn't say fly, I said *tell them to fly*. The attempt alone will get our speed up even more. Their problem isn't they can't get fast enough to fly, it's that there's too much weight in here to get airborne.' Dash explained, only partly making sense to Santa, but he complied anyway.

He yelled and screamed and fired words at the reindeer that were far too strange for me to spell here, and as he continued to wave the leather reins about, they felt a solid but smooth tug right through their bodies, and the reindeer began to glide across the ice. The back few were still making solid contact with the surface of the river, but those at the front of their team were dancing through the air a few inches above it, dragging the nose of the sleigh up slightly, as their speed became far greater than Aiden ever imagined possible.

The sleigh bounced about, up and down, as the reindeer had trouble coordinating themselves in this odd and unusual task, with the front of the sleigh popping up a bit, then the weight of its overloaded occupants bouncing it back down, slamming onto the ice and tugging those flying few reindeer back down a bit, before they would jerk it forward again.

'Fly!' Dan yelled, seeing a huge, cracked section of ice straight in front of them sticking up in the air like a skateboard ramp. He knew very well they were not going to fly; they had already proven that impossible in the current situation, but he said it anyway.

Santa pushed his feet into the floor in front of him and leaned back hard into his seat, yelling more strange orders at the reindeer and waving the reins about in a panic.

The sleigh was too much for the now separated sheet of ice to hold, and it broke right through into the freezing water, which was flowing surprisingly fast down there. Santa continued to yell and swing his arms about, nearly knocking those close by out of the sleigh, and the reindeer pulled, getting as close to flight as they possibly could as they dragged the sleigh through the water behind them like a skier behind a boat.

The cracking didn't stop there. As they continued to be dragged upstream, forcing their way up the ice, the bottom of the sleigh ploughed through the frozen river, smashing the ice under its weight as the cracks in the separating sheets seemed to be chasing them.

Santa yelled as they continued upstream, like he still thought there was some chance of flying out of the situation, as Aiden and the elves held on to both the sleigh and each other in hope of keeping themselves from falling into the water. Even arms as thick and muscular as Santa's get tired eventually, and after so much waving of those reins, he began to slow. At first it was like the giving up type of slowing and he half expected them to sink through the ice as his energy ran out, but to his pleasant surprise it was more of a dropping back into a rhythm that worked, and they began to glide across the top of the water a little more gracefully. They were still smashing up a trail of crushed ice as they went, but they were now doing so with a continuous and powerful pull, and instead of fighting to get airborne, they were putting their energy into moving forward through the ice.

This continued for quite a while, with many of the elves surprised by the endurance of the reindeer to maintain such an energetic pull as they went around a few more bends and through a couple of slightly concerning rocky sections, making it through without incident.

Now the forest began to change. After hours of travelling up the ice like this, it was late in the day and the sun was disappearing behind the tree-covered hills, but even before this, the forest was becoming dark, with less life.

'These trees don't look well.' Coop said, having never been this far upstream or seen this part of the forest before. The leaves weren't dead, and the branches hadn't dried out, but they just looked bad. The pine needles weren't about to fall off or becoming brittle, but they were going black, and the further they continued up toward The Black Rock, the blacker they became, until the river was soon lined with trees that were completely horrible.

No one responded to him, and he added to his comment. 'It's like they're the same trees, but different. They look like the pine trees around home, but black. What's wrong with them, Dash?' he asked, directing the question to someone specific in hope of a response.

'I don't know Coop. They never used to be like this.' came the quiet response.

'What happened to them?'

'I don't know, mate. Dolph says it happened when Krampus took his first victims all those years ago. Then as time passed and he took more and more, the black infection grew, then stayed like this all that time he was gone.' Dash explained as best he could.

'So, what happens now that he's back? Will it spread through the forest further?'

'No idea Coop. Your guess is as good as mine.' Dash replied with a shake of the head as Aiden put a hand on his shoulder and stood up, turning and pointing to the peak up ahead in front of them. 'This is it, isn't it?' he asked, certain he was correct.

Santa looked up at him over his shoulder solemnly. 'That's The Black Rock Aiden.' Then they heard one hell of a roar, which everyone except Aiden knew for sure to be a dragon;

a big one, and though it was just as likely to have come from the sky far above them, they all willed the sleigh to move just a little faster, fearing for little Sophie, imprisoned at The Black Rock.

16

As they turned the corner, Dash pointed to a flattish spot at the river's edge where the bank tapered off down toward the level of the ice, and an old and unused path branched off. 'What do you think, guys? Drag this thing up onto land?' he suggested to Dan and Santa by his side.

Dan nodded back at him. 'Yeah, I don't like the look of how this river has turned. I think we'll all feel much safer on solid ground.' Santa agreed, and Dan added 'Solid ground with a bit of cover.' looking around them in all directions, feeling very much like they could be attacked at any moment and thinking about how little they could do to protect themselves.

The second the reindeer dragged the sleigh clear of the ice and onto the hard, dark brown ground, they collapsed in a heap. The elves climbed out of the sleigh and checked them over, offering them some food from the supply of fruit and vegetables they still had in the back to feed themselves, which they all accepted with complete gratitude.

Aiden jumped down and walked to the front of the group, past Santa who was standing in deep conversation with Dash, Dan and Blitz, pointing up the track and working toward agreement for their next move. He looked at them as he passed and reached for the handle by his left wrist, ripped his sword out of the sheath with a fast tug, and continued up the hill toward his sister. When he got about twenty or thirty metres past the group talking tactics, he heard his name called and turned to look back at them.

'What?'

'Aiden, where are you going?' Dan asked simply, knowing he couldn't possibly survive up there alone.

'What does it look like? I'm going to get my sister.'

'Alright mate, just cool it for a minute and give us some time to have a plan.' Santa said, then turned away from him and back to his little group of leaders.

'A plan.' he mumbled to himself dismissively, almost mocking Santa's comment and preferring action. He turned and started walking again.

'Aiden!' Dan shouted sharply when he saw him walking away again, in a way that told Aiden he was being firm but also being the friend he had become to the young man.

He stopped and looked back at them over his shoulder, not bothering to turn right back around, allowing his body language to declare his intent to continue in a few seconds, so they better speak up.

'Give us a chance, mate. Just running up there and charging in is how we get ourselves killed. Five minutes to discuss a strategy can be the difference between success and failure here mate, this is not our first time doing this stuff. Come down here and join us if you like, but either way just wait.' Dan pleaded, explaining himself as well as he could, and inviting him into the discussion, which turned out to be the part that changed Aiden's mind.

He walked back down the path and became part of their little circle, and the conversation continued from where they were before he distracted them.

'Forget about the dragon, we haven't seen it at all, and haven't heard another sound out of it since the roar back down there.' Blitz stated.

'Yes, but that doesn't mean it's not a threat.' Dash argued, playing the overly cautions role as usual.

'No, you're right, it doesn't, but we can't plan around it. Forget about it.'

'Forget about a damn dragon, Blitzen?' Dash shot back, raising his voice.

'Yes, that's right, you're finally getting it. When a dragon presents itself in front of us, we will react to it, but not before.'

'You'll kill us all with that attitude.' Dash started until Santa raised a palm to stop him.

'He's right, you know Dash. We only heard it. It could have been flying away from here, or just passing over. That's not unheard of around here.' he explained rather logically.

They all glanced around at each other looking for truce in the other's eyes, and Dan spoke, seeing Aiden's agitation at the time wasting. 'Alright, let's talk about what we can control. It looks like the entrance to The Rock itself isn't as far up the mountain as we thought"",' he started as they all turned to look up the track. 'Let's get moving up there, I think we can go on foot.'

'Yeah, I agree, we can move in pretty quietly on foot; a few archers, put some good shields up front, we can sneak in ready for a fight.' Santa said.

'Those reindeer aren't pulling that load any further, anyway.' Dash added, nodding back down toward the resting animals. 'We'll lead the way up and have a couple of elves lead them up after a bit of a rest.

'Alright, let's do it.' Aiden said as he turned and marched back down the hill toward the sleigh and the rest of the elves. The boy was very impatient, which annoyed some, but Santa was quietly becoming very impressed with his growing leadership and no-nonsense attitude. He went straight to the back of the sleigh and grabbed a shield, then started walking back up the hill.

'Vick and Comet,' Santa called out across the scattering of elves and reindeer on the path, then continued when they both turned to look at him. 'I need you two to lead the reindeer up with the sleigh. Everyone else, arm yourself and come with me.' he said and turned to start back up the track, where Dash and Blitz were already moving. . They were led up there by a stubbornly determined Aiden, calling over his shoulder for the rest of them to hurry.

Catching up to Aiden, Dan was quickly able to talk him around and slow him down for long enough to let the rest of the team catch up.

With shields raised and arrows pointed to the path ahead, they marched on in a tight group, protecting Aiden in the middle of them. As they entered each corner, a couple of them would creep in against the rock walls first to check for threats as they approached each new section, but every time, to their surprise, they were just coming into empty path after empty path.

'I expected better security than this.' Santa whispered after a while to no one in particular.

'Hm, perhaps the reputation of this place has outgrown its reality.' Blitz offered.

They continued like this until they were nearly at the top, 'Wolves.' Santa stated calmly as they made their way around the corner right into Krampus' front yard and saw three huge black wolves running at them as if all they were was prey.

Like the well-trained machine they had become, they fired arrows in a flowing sequence, reloading in the seconds covered by other's shots, with each arrow finding its bullseye, dropping the wolves to the ground with a crashing thud.

Those of the elves who hadn't seen The Black Rock before, nearly all of them, looked around, amazed. It wasn't really all that impressive, but the mythology of the place had made it such that anything would have been fascinating; it could have been a giant teapot and that would have still been amazing to them, but as the name would suggest, it was a black rock, a very big black rock.

The path they were on had taken them up onto the huge open platform that led to the entry gates. For something so simple, it was a brilliant piece of strategic design. It was like having a vacant stone football field between the path and the gates, forcing anyone that approached to completely expose themselves to the guards on their way in. On one side of the big stone slab was a vertical cliff that dropped hundreds of metres to the black forest below, and the only thing on the other side of it was The Rock. There was the rock face of the entry, with the thick iron gateway carved into the centre, then the mountain above it, with the two merging somewhere high into the clouds. Out by the ""cliff's edge was a steel platform fixed to the rock wall at each side, with enough room for a couple of guards. There was a ladder on each, both broken, though one was worse than the other. Neither had handrails or anything else to stop them falling off the side, and most strangely, no guards present at all.

As they took the corner, Blitz pulled hard on his bow,

expecting an ambush, and moved his arm across the centre of the space before them, then up to the platform to the right. He pulled himself in against the left wall to protect against any possible attack from the other side and looked around carefully.

He waited, with his arrow ready to fire, concentrating as he waited for movement, then loosened the pressure and gestured to Dan, asking, 'See anything?' in a quiet whisper.

He shook his head in response, then shifted his eyes across to Santa. 'Nothing. The place is unguarded. Weird.' And they stepped out into the open.

Santa led the team on from there, taking the first few steps tentatively, looking around with his shield raised as he considered the chance of a surprise attack from far above, which did not come.

'This is very strange,' he said out loud and continued as he looked around for enemies. 'I'd actually feel much more comfortable if something would just come on out and attack us, at least then we know what's happening. This just doesn't make sense.'

'Where are they? I don't understand.' Dash added in a whisper, like he was just thinking out loud.

'Who cares? As long as Sophie's here,' Aiden butted in as he pushed through to the front of the group and added, 'Come on, let's go.' and began jogging toward the heavy iron gates.

Santa's reflexes had him throw out an arm to stop him, which was too slow anyway, but he then thought about it again, and decided the kid may not be in the wrong at all. The place certainly did appear very empty, so empty that Santa thought the idea of allowing the bold march forward through the vast exposed courtyard may not be as silly as it sounds.

'Let's go get your sister back.' he said to Aiden as he

jogged up to his side. They were both running now, toward the intimidating iron gates and the shadows beyond their slight opening, with the rest of the group following slightly behind them on a high alert, with weapons raised and eyes moving around searching for danger.

Aiden looked at Santa running at his right shoulder from the corner of his eye and grinned. They were still in a bad situation with no idea of what waited for them in the shadows ahead, or whether Sophie was going to be alright, but his grin was a reflection of things lighter than this. He felt pride in how he had changed in recent days, become stronger, more resilient and surer of himself, with the leadership he had observed in Santa becoming part of him. He was scared, of course he was. He was scared for his little sister, and he had no idea of the danger that could be near, but what he could now do was overcome this fear and act with confidence. That was what the grin was about, and to have Santa see this in him gave Aiden a great feeling.

He nodded to himself, then swung his right arm out and smacked Santa in the middle of his thick gorilla chest with a playful backhand, then reached for the sword at his left wrist. 'Yeah, let's go get her back.'

Santa smiled back for a second and drew a sword in each hand, tapping one against Aiden's gently in a high five type gesture, and looked to the darkness ahead of them behind the slightly ajar picket gateway.

17

'Light it up Blitzen.' Santa said over his shoulder, making a bit of space between himself and Aiden, and pointing a sword through the gates.

There was a clicking sound and the solid knock of metal, then the glow of fire coming from back in Blitz's direction. The flaming arrow flew out of the group, between Aiden and Santa, and through the open gates into the dark cavernous room.

They saw little from this first arrow other than the room was wide, high, and mostly empty. There were some shallow lines cut into the floor like the spaces between giant cold floor tiles, and a huge chandelier that looked like it could have been the wheel of a wagon they had destroyed, hung in the middle of the ceiling between beams and rafters. There was something in the middle of the back wall; possibly a single piece of furniture, but it was very hard to see exactly what it was from outside under such poor light.

'Still can't see much.' Santa said slowly as he squinted his eyes to try and see more, reaching one hand out to Aiden's elbow to slow him down.

'We'll see plenty when we get in there.' was Aiden's stubborn response as he pulled his arm away from Santa's loose grip and pushed forward.

'Want me to break one up in there?' Blitz offered, drawing another arrow and attaching something to its head before lighting it on fire.

'Please.' Santa accepted, gesturing him to proceed, and again nudging Aiden to allow the team to work together.

The arrow flew between the gates much like before, but popped up slightly higher than the first one, then came down and burst on the floor in the centre of the room. Little chunks of fire slid across the floor in all directions, splashing a low red glow over everything as far back as the rear wall and as wide as both side walls, leaving only the ceiling in the dark.

There against the back wall, right in the centre, they saw the single piece of furniture they couldn't quite work out under the lower light. It was a big old dirty iron throne, and chained to it, balled up on the floor to its side, was Sophie.

Aiden saw her and it was like every muscle in his body jumped at once. A pained gasp flew from his mouth, and he took off in a desperate sprint to her. 'Sophie.' he screamed, and she lifted her face toward him as Santa and the elves ran to catch up.

'Aiden!' came the sobbing scream that burst from her little body, exhausted and scared.

'I'm coming.' he yelled as he passed through the spiked gates and crossed the floor toward her.

The air seemed to change as he entered the room and left the crisp, frosty air from outside. The smell was strange. It was one of moisture that never leaves, or mould and stagnant filth, something old and dead, and something else that reminded him of the old fish tank in the shed mum kept telling dad to get rid of.

Sophie's face was beetroot red, and her eyes were puffy and swollen, dripping with tears. She looked like she had been rolled in coal, then dragged through prickle bushes. Her clothes were torn, she was missing a shoe, and there was a rusty dish of water a few feet from where she was curled up, like she was being fed like a dog. A heavy round iron bracket was attached to her ankle, similar to a boat mooring, and a chain as thick as her arm with an  ancient-looking padlock secured her to the throne.

The giant metal throne looked more like a statue than a real piece of furniture. It was thick and bulky and looked as heavy as an elephant, but twice as hard. It was black, with rust covering any parts that weren't black, and it dripped with a strange black sludge. The arms were thick and flat on top, with rolled over ends on the front that looked like two monstrous arms with clenched fists holding things in place.

A slimy black monitor dragon dropped down from above and landed between Aiden and his little sister. He grimaced at the sound as it landed, which he thought must have hurt it, but it showed no signs of any pain as its thick, round belly and tail smacked against the stone tiles. It raised its head and hissed at him, baring its sharp teeth, which were so filthy they made Aiden immediately want to find a bathroom and brush his own.

With his sword already in one hand, and a shield in the other, he stopped and steadied himself, watching the animal to see what it was going to do. He felt Santa arrive behind him, heard his feet crunch on the grains of broken rock in the tile joints, then his puffing breath. 'Move aside mate, I'll sort this out.' he said, pushing past Aiden with a large axe in his hands. Aiden had never seen the axe before and had no idea where it had come from.

The dragon stood tall on its hind legs, balanced by its powerful tail, and opened its mouth wide, roaring a loud and foul-smelling blast at their faces. Its front feet had come right up by its head and flexed in anger, its claws growing with agitation.

Santa reacted on instinct and grabbed Aiden's shoulder, shoving him out of the way. The beast was coming at him fast now, but as it jumped through the air to attack, it was met by the head of Santa's heavy axe.

'Oww.' Aiden said from the floor with his hand on his back after tripping when Santa pushed past him.

'Get up.' Santa said unsympathetically, knowing it was just a bump. 'You'll be fine.'

He got up and turned his attention back toward Sophie. 'It's alright, it's alright. I'm here now.' He whispered as he slid across the floor to her on his knees and used his own body to cover as much of her as he could as she cried into his chest, unsure of what else could be around.

'Are you alright? Are you hurt?' He asked as he held her face in both hands and looked into her eyes.

Santa stood over them, looking around, and the elves began to arrive, surrounding them with shields raised and taut bows at the ready as they looked around the rest of the room.

'I'm alright.' she squeaked.

'Are you sure?' Aiden asked again, feeling and checking her then sticking the end of his sword into the lock and twisting it with a click as it unlocked to release her, without even considering the incredible fact the sword had just shrunk to the size he needed to do this, just as Santa had said it would.

'Yeah, don't worry about me.' she repeated, then added 'I'm just hungry.' Which made Aiden and a few of the elves laugh.

Santa wasn't in a mood to laugh; he felt very uneasy about being there at all and was just as concerned about how strangely empty the place was. 'Where's Krampus?' he asked Sophie seriously.

'I don't know. They left a long time ago.' she spoke.

'To go where?'

'I don't know. Why would they tell me? I just heard him say something about a plan to go after some wizard, then they just took off.' She said, not realising the significance of the statement, then turned to her brother and added, 'Who are these people, Aiden?'.

'What?' Santa snapped, rushing in to closely hear her explain herself.

'Aiden, who is this man?' she sobbed into her brother's sleeve from within a secure hug.

He looked down at her red and dirty face and tried to explain, though he knew how silly it would sound. 'This is Santa, Soph.'

'Wait, what?' came her confused response, having

thought she must have misheard him, though she didn't expect it was a time for his silliness.

'I know it sounds weird, but trust me, this is what Santa really is, the stories of him are all wrong.' he explained, knowing the interruption was coming.

'What did Krampus say Sophie? Tell me exactly what you heard. This is important.' the big man asked intensely, trying not to scare her any more than she already was.

She was intimidated by this bearded mad man questioning her, and recoiled as he spoke at her, coming closer and closer to her as he went on. 'I don't know. He just said they were going after some great wizard or something. And something about taking the power of someone. I don't know, it didn't make sense.' she finished vaguely, hoping it would be enough for the man to leave her alone.

'Who?' Santa asked as soon as she finished, then went on when she didn't instantly respond, 'Who was the wizard he was talking about? Give me a name.'

She started to cry, and squeaked a few words 'I don't know, I can't remember.' she said.

'Think!' he yelled at her, prompting Aiden to raise a firm hand and tell him to back off, before he came back for another gentler go, 'This is important Sophie, so please try to remember the name.'

She sniffed and wiped her eyes, then sat up a bit, pulling herself out of Aiden's protective arms. 'I'm really not sure, but it might have been Ralph, or something like that. But that doesn't sound wizard-like at all. I'm sorry, I just don't know.' she finished, as Santa cut in over her words.

'Was it Rudolph?' he asked flatly, dreading what now seemed obvious.

'Yes, that's it.' she began, but as soon as he saw the recognition in her eyes, Santa interrupted her again, barking orders like a military general with no time to waste talking about it any longer.

'Get her out of here.' he began pointing at Sophie as he stood up and walked away toward the gates, then yelled across the stone court outside, 'Vick, Comet, get the sleigh up here. We're leaving now.' Shouting the final word in a booming voice that echoed off the hard surfaces around them.

18

Aiden turned his attention back to his little sister after watching Santa march away, handing out orders, and she got up and chased after him as he took her by the hand and ran out of there.

'We both know we're not flying back, not all of us.' Dash started the conversation as he rushed to keep up with Santa's long-legged strides.

'Not all of us, that's right.' came the response.

'The kids can't stay here. We need to get them into the sleigh and headed for The Pole.' Dash suggested.

'Yes. They'll come with me. So will Dan, Rance and Blitz. That's it, any more will slow us down too much. We need to get to Dolph.' he said, looking to his trusted friend with worried eyes. 'I don't know how, Dash, but I need you to lead the rest of the elves home.'

Dash nodded his head and agreed, unsure of how they would go about it, but knew they'd find a way.

They rushed back out into the open stone entry as the

reindeer dragged the sleigh up and around the corner in front of them. Santa was happy to risk it with the gargoyles if they were still up there. He doubted they would be, considering there was literally almost nothing left for them to guard.

He needed as much power and speed as possible, which meant keeping all eight reindeer pulling the sleigh, and the difficult but quick decision had to be made to leave elves behind with no reindeer or anything else but each other to get them back. Yes, he was abandoning them, but they understood it was necessary if they were to save Dolph and the other elves back at The Pole.

'Stay out of the forest. I don't know what the alternative is, but the hundreds of trolls, wolves and ground dragons that are normally up here with Krampus must be somewhere, and I'm tipping that if he flew over to miss us, everything else was probably sent into the forest to stop us.'

'Agreed.' Dash replied, looking thoughtfully into the distance. 'Don't worry about it, you go. We'll work ourselves out.'

He stopped and pointed at Dash firmly. 'We'll meet you there.' he spoke.

Santa left with the sleigh, the reindeer, three elves and Aiden and Sophie, and the remaining five had nothing to do but take the first steps back toward The Pole and see what happened from there. This meant back down the way they came, but they were quickly reminded it led to nothing but the river, which was now awash with smashed up chunks of ice. What only an hour earlier had been a flat and calm smooth white ice surface with the power of the flowing water down beneath it, had now become a totally wild blast of ice chunks. All that power of the water that had been contained to that hidden compartment under the ice was now flexing its muscles and showing its destructive hurry to move downstream.

19

The small group left behind quickly made their way back down to the river, and as the flurry of broken ice sheets came into view between the old, blackened trees, Dash looked around the group. They were all thinking the same thing; they had a wild ride ahead.

They skidded to a stop at the water's edge, which was splashing all over the place now in its blasting flow. Dash put his hands on his hips and looked up the river as far as he could see to the next bend. 'I don't think we have any other option, elves. We're going to have to make a raft.' he declared.

'And put it on that?' asked Vick with a nervous giggle. 'It'll be smashed to pieces before the next bend.'

'If you've got a better idea, I'd love to hear it.' he replied seriously.

'We've got no sleigh, no reindeer, and other than this river, which does literally go to our front door, the only other option is to walk back.' Coop pointed out.

'That'll take days, weeks even.' Vick added.

'That's time we don't have. They're on the way back to fight Krampus and who knows how many of his troll mates, and they need us. The river is our fastest way home. No doubt.' Coop stated with confidence.

'Yes, that's great to say, but we won't be of any use to them if our raft gets smashed into a pile of ice on the way, will we?!' Vick snapped emotionally, with fear becoming visible in her eyes. 'I say we take the walk through the forest, and at least we get there.'

'I think she might be right. Not ideal, I know, but it makes sense.' Comet supplied.

Coop was getting frustrated at the time wasting, and he paced across the path along the river's edge then paused to look at Dash, who could silently see they were both thinking the same thing, though Dash was just standing back and observing the conversation. 'Did you not hear what Santa said back there? The hundreds of trolls, wolves, ground dragons, and take a guess at what else, are all out there in that forest somewhere, and they'll be doing two things; heading toward The Pole to help Krampus and looking for us. We are not going through that forest.' he said firmly, clearly becoming angry.

They all spoke at once now and the squabbling continued for a few minutes, going nowhere and achieving nothing more than making a lot of noise. Then Dash spoke loudly, demanding their attention as he slammed his sword into the ground angrily. 'Quiet! Stop your arguing. We are wasting time while Santa and the others are probably flying right into an all-out fight to survive, and I only hope Dolph is ok. Just stop it,' he repeated, spitting with rage. 'We will not be going into that forest, that's final,' Then he turned and pointed his sword at the river. 'This is our ride home. Now, everyone gathers around close and be ready to move,' he continued, confusing almost all of them, then turned to Coop. 'Lead the way, young elf.' And he stood back and pointed both arms toward the churning river like a gentleman letting someone pass through an open door before him.

Coop took off running toward the water, his eyes focused on one particular piece of ice approaching from upstream. He reached the edge and threw himself into the air, landing on the passing slab of ice. He slipped halfway across it, then stabbed his sword into it a little way to give himself a sort of handle to hang onto, and turned to look back at the rest of the group.

'All aboard,' he yelled with a mischievous grin, not giving anyone a chance to object or offer a better idea before taking off down the river.

Dash moved next, taking a few quick steps backward then sprinting into his run up as he watched his target ice raft approach, and jumped, adding a pole vault action with his sword, and landed awkwardly on his ride, sinking his weapon in for a handle too. He looked up to see Comet flying through the air toward him. 'Come on you lot, get moving.' he yelled back upriver to those remaining on the bank, whose faces ranged from scared to excited, but once the first of them jumped, they all followed one after the other, and they each boarded their little ice boats and took off down the water, speeding toward home.

20

The flight back to The Pole for Santa and those with him in the sleigh took a small fraction of the time taken the other way, with the speed of the sky being used with a fearless desperation that came with worry for the old elvish wizard. Dolph was certainly every bit the legend his reputation would have you believe, and still possessed great magical power, but it couldn't be denied that as an old man he was certainly not what he used to be. There's the magic used to help Santa along with his Christmas trip around the world and other simple tricks. Then there's the magic needed to physically win a fight, and they are just not the same. Dolph was an old wizard, and though he could certainly do some damage, it would not be wise for him to take Krampus on at his age. But Santa also knew very well Dolph would not be willing to stand aside for his own sake, while Krampus went after the younger elves who had stayed home with him and weren't trained to defend themselves at all.

Santa cracked the reins through the cold air, again yelling the strange words he used when urging the reindeer on, in a language that seemed to the two kids to be less like a language every time they heard it, and more like made up gibberish. Whatever it was, and I'm sure Dash would be able to explain the history of it if they ever get the chance to ask him later, it was working very well. The speeds they were now traveling at were faster than any of them had ever seen anything go, with the children holding on with white knuckled fear, and even the elves feeling quite uncomfortable.

A dark column of smoke rose straight up from in front of the main building. It was visible long before anything else, and as they got close and their eyes followed it down, they found it to be coming from the crops, the hay sheds, and even the old windmill which was somehow still turning, with the four blades appearing like a fire spinning circus trick.

Though the exact source of some of it may not have been clear yet, there was also smoke rising in misty and less focused areas all over the place, with a lot over the main building. There was significant damage, with a huge section of the roof completely smashed in like something very big had crashed right through it; something the elves assumed, and Santa was near certain, was a dragon.

Santa's grim face turned to each of the elves and he said nothing. No words. The emotion written on his face said enough. Anger, fear for their loved ones, and sadness for the undoubted loss they had taken. Dan broke their stare after a few seconds, gave his dear friend a firm pat on the back that would have knocked a regular sized man off the front of the seat, and said, 'We'll fight back. We can recover from this.' And looked away.

Santa just grunted inaudibly and nodded his head, then followed Dan's eyes to the edge of the forest where he was

watching crowds of trolls and other harder to identify creatures march across the grassy hills like protesters storming
toward city hall.

'Call off the search, we found the trolls,' Dan said with
a shake of the head, then looked around the group, 'Is it
just me, of are you guys feeling more and more like we've
been played?'

'Hmm.' Santa groaned, annoyed at himself for not thinking of this earlier.

'That whole time, from when we passed a few of them in
the forest, to finding The Rock near empty, they were headed
here. How could we be so stupid?' Dash talked himself
through, yelling in anger by the end.

'Yes, stupid indeed. We've been fooled. Right from when
he took Sophie, it was just a plan to make us leave The Pole
unguarded,' Santa said into his hands, with his head slumped
toward his feet.

'That may be, but we had to save her. We couldn't just
leave her there. You did the right thing.' Aiden contributed
from over the back.

'No, you don't understand. I have underestimated him
completely. I think this was his intention all along. Krampus
didn't just realise we would be sending our best team away
from The Pole to get Sophie back, it was the reason he took
her in the first place, and it's why he did it just as I showed
up to chase them. None of it was an accident. This all happened so he could have his best shot at Dolph.' he explained
as he stood up and whacked the front of the sleigh hard in
anger with the flat side of his sword. When he set it all out
like this, they all knew he was right.

They all went quiet for a few moments as the wheels of
thought spun in their minds, and Blitz noticed another small

army of trolls marching in from the other side of the river, like ants crawling over a new piece of territory.

He stood up and turned the crossbow that was still in place, mounted on the front of the sleigh, and began checking it over, preparing it to throw steel at whatever was in their way. 'Any of the big arrows left back there, Rance?' he asked, pivoting toward where she had moved to check on Sophie.

'Yeah there's a few.' she replied, passing a handful to him, and he loaded them into place.

One thing they all noticed as they got closer was they couldn't see any elves, and though this didn't mean they were safe, it did mean there was hope. They weren't out fighting or hurt in the fields. The elves left there were mostly very young, very old, and those just expected to not do well in battle. You know, like bakers; there has never been a single elvish baker that could fight, and the same could be said for quilters, carpenters, and farrier elves; but we all have our purpose.

Santa was sure they would have known what to do; As long as they knew the attack was coming in sufficient time, Dolph would have ensured their safety. Yes, he may be old, but a wizard of his great experience and power does not simply shrivel with age and become something less. As long as the elves were all able to get there, and Dolph didn't have to direct his attention toward a fight of any kind to defend them, he could guide them; Santa knew the old wizard would have led them all into the tunnels and away to safety.

It broke Santa's heart to see the place like this. Broken, infested, taken, and full of evil, fear and dread. He knew the elves inside relied on him to provide safety, and with it, happiness, but they now had neither. He looked down and felt the terror they must all be plagued by, and felt to have personally failed them all, his heart stinging at the feeling of having let them down so badly.

'We've got dramas up here big guy.' Blitz said, nodding his head toward a group of gargoyles in front of them.

'Damn it, Blitzen.' he blasted, though it obviously wasn't any fault of Blitz.

'Yeah, who'd have guessed they'd be here guarding us from our own home.'

Santa didn't know what to do when he saw them approaching, and as he watched them coming closer, he just stared blankly at them like he was just hoping the solution would come to him. He had never defeated a pack of this size, and as he stared vacantly, thinking it over, the sleigh slowed to a benign drift.

Blitz shook him out of it, putting a firm hand on his shoulder from behind him. 'Speed up!' he said with certainty.

'What?' Santa responded, confused.

'Go faster.'

'And when we get to them?' he replied again like he had just heard the stupidest comment in the world, 'Then what?'

'Just hit them hard; we're bound to hurt a few,' Blitz said to a very unsure Santa, then turned to Dan and Rance looking for their support, 'We'll jump on whatever isn't taken out by us smashing this thing into them and ride them to the ground while you go on,' he finished with a smile, like he had just proposed something totally normal, then added 'But hopefully we can just smash through them without getting to that point.' Looking like he understood the madness of what he just said.

'Oh god, he's insane,' Santa sighed with one hand over his face, then paused for a moment, looked up and roared a booming 'Hoo!' at the reindeer and drove them to hit these things as hard as they could.

Smashing straight through the pack of the beasts, they rushed forward, descending quickly, far quicker than intended, and with little control. There was one gargoyle caught up on one of the bars coming off the reindeers' harness chassis, struggling to free itself. It was very badly wounded and had no chance of being able to fly under its own power.

The drag of this extra weight on the front, as well as now having at least two badly injured reindeer, was making flight very difficult as they dove faster and harder toward the ground, and what was expected to be a dangerous landing.

'Dan.' Rance yelled from the back of the sleigh. He turned to the sight of her fighting off another of the beasts that been able to grab hold as they smashed through. It had the claws of its feet latched onto the back rail and was swapping blows with the young elf.

'Alright, I'm coming.' he shouted back as he pulled an arrow to his bow and released it quickly, sending the creature flying off the sleigh to the ground below.

Knowing the coming crash landing would almost certainly hurt the reindeer if it caused the sleigh to flip and land on top of them, Santa disconnected them. He waited until they had carried the sleigh as far as they could and the ground was only a short fall away, and he pulled the pin, releasing all eight reindeer to land with only themselves to worry about, and one persistent gargoyle to trample.

The sleigh hit the track between paddocks, bounced through a fence, smashed the chook house to splinters on the way through, and spun to a stop behind the bushy hedges of the usually beautiful outdoor dining area. Despite their injuries and the madness of the scene around them, they piled out of the sleigh the moment it stopped, and took cover behind the old stone barbeque, protecting Sophie in the centre of the group.

Red faced and breathing heavy, they crouched in an exhausted pile behind the short stone wall and tried to take in the state of the place that was normally so peaceful and perfect. There was already significant damage, and Krampus was there somewhere, but the most obvious thing to them all was that they had still not seen a single elf.

21

Sheltered behind their little stone wall, they had no idea just how close the group they left back at The Black Rock was getting, and how quickly and recklessly they approached.

The rushing flow of chilled water drove them downstream toward home with the speed they wanted, but also the danger they did not. They bumped and ground together like old bumper cars, raising fear of falling off with the first few bumps, before they became more relaxed as they got used to it.

The elves all knew it when they heard the roar, and Vick turned straight to Coop and yelled, 'Yes, that's the sound of a waterfall. Great plan.'

Coop just laughed, 'It's still safer than the forest.'

'We'll be fine.' Dash began, seeing the need to calm some worried elves, having taken notice of this waterfall in the past, and already considered the upcoming descent.

'You think?' came the sarcastic response.

'Yes. Well, I'm pretty sure,' he went on, looking around and speaking loudly to the group who were now scattered over a large area of river. 'I've certainly never been over it on a chunk of ice, but I think we'll be ok. It's more the speed of the flow that's the issue, rather than the height of the fall.'

'If we're going to drown in ice water, I don't care whether it's the speed or the fall that causes it; the freaking waterfall is the problem.' Comet contributed, looking worried, triggering everyone else to throw in their comments, and they all started yelling at each other, arguing for or against something they were now powerless to stop, anyway.

'Shut up. All of you,' Dash yelled, with a frustrated look on his face that demanded better cooperation and thought, 'We're going over it whether you like it or not. Just hold on and get as low to your ice as you can, keep upright, and I'll see you all on that nice calm wide river waiting on the other side.' And on they went, submitting to the leader of the group, and the power of the river that was about to throw them a little closer to home.

22

'Where is everyone?' Dan asked as Santa and Blitz poked their heads out over the end of the wall and looked up the hill toward the building a short distance away.

'I don't know, mate,' Santa replied hopefully. 'With Dolph, somewhere. No dead or injured, not a scream or call for help, just nothing. That's classic Rudolph. He would have taken them into the tunnels under the mountain.' he explained, sounding proud of his old friend's predictable brilliance.

'I hope you're right, but couldn't the elves have gone into the tunnels without him?' Blitz wondered.

'No, they couldn't have. They wouldn't know the way. Very few of us even know where the entry is. They're with him, I have no doubt.'

'Alright let's go then.' Dan said, looking around with an arrow drawn to his bow, anxious to get moving. They did have the cover of the stone barbeque area protecting them from one side, but he was very conscious of the fact anything coming from down toward the river or over the hill toward The Black Rock direction would see them very clearly, which could force them to choose between pushing back to fight or retreating into the building ahead.

Santa stuck his head up again to look to their route in toward the tunnels, via a door that lay smashed in at the top of the gently curved path, paved from the same stone as their current checkpoint. 'Straight up here,' he began, pointing to the damaged opening, 'I'm hoping that whatever didn't like our door is gone. We head for the main dining hall, then take the door at the back near the courtyard into that long corridor out to Dolph's cabin.'

'Hold on,' Blitz interjected, ducking back into cover and looking at Santa. 'We're assuming Krampus hasn't found the tunnels, right?'

'Yeah.' Santa confirmed.

'So why don't we go after him instead. Just take him out directly instead of protecting his target. Be aggressive, not defensive.'

'We don't know where he is, but we can take a pretty good guess at where the elves are. It just makes sense to go to them first, then defend from there.' Dan explained.

'Defend? Look around you Dan, there's not much left to defend. And you saw the number of trolls about to arrive. This is the time to attack, that's how we save what's left of the place; the elves.' Blitz hissed angrily, trying to keep to a whisper, but slipping toward a yell.

Santa turned to them both to sort it out, 'We can't take these two to a fight against Krampus, that would be crazy.' he said, nodding toward the two kids.

'Yeah agreed, no way. We need to get them to the safety of the tunnels.' Rance agreed.

'Alright, we make a rush for the tunnels, we drop the kids

off to hide there with Dolph, and we go after him before the rest of his army turns up.' Santa said.

'Oh my God, what is that smell?' Aiden gasped, reaching his hand over his nose and gagging into it as the most offensively foul odour invaded his senses.

'Trolls.' Santa reacted, turning his eyes over the top of the stone again as Blitz did the same and Dan crept up at Santa's shoulder with an arrow drawn to his bow, ready to fly.

A troll walked out of the broken doorway casually, bumping into the jamb on the way through, and looked around blankly, like it had no idea why it existed at all. It was as if it had nothing to do and was looking out over the scenery, like a tourist gazing out to sea from a hotel balcony. It raised a half-eaten leg of ham to its mouth and took a bite, then discarded it, throwing it randomly into the garden down the hill.

As it turned to go back inside, probably to further pillage the pantry, Rance tripped as she led the kids closer into the shelter of the wall. The troll stopped and turned around at the sound, drawing a weapon at its hip as it went, but was met by an arrow from Dan's bow, dropping it to the ground right where it stood.

The sound of a troll hitting the ground is not a soft or delicate thing, and a second of the beasts very quickly appeared in the doorway to check the noise. It stepped into the opening, looked down at the body at its feet with an arrow sticking out of it, raised its eyes to look for the source of the attack, and fell.

'How stupid are they?' Aiden said with his head now also popping up over the wall to watch both Dan and Blitz sink arrows into the second troll, dropping it onto the first.

'Very.' Santa replied, 'But we should move on, there could be hundreds more of them around here, and it won't all be that easy.' And he ducked out from the end of the wall, ran through the garden and onto the path that led to the door and the pile of dead troll.

'Hey dopey.' he said out loud, then threw one of his short swords expertly into an invisible bullseye on the chest of a third troll that was now making its way toward the door as Santa glanced inside.

The foul smell coming off the lumpy pile of troll in the doorway was very distracting, and one most of them hadn't smelled this close before. Blitz stepped around them and through the doorway past Santa, taking the lead in this next stage of the careful entry. Shuffling along the wall to the corner, he paused for Dan to come in and mirror him on the opposite wall, and they swung around the corner into the empty hall with tense arrows raised, each covering one end of the room.

23

The air was clear, with no rotten smell of trolls in the hall, other than the traces wafting from outside, and Dan turned to signal to Santa that it was safe to bring the others through.

'Lock the doors, boys.' Santa requested as he walked in, looking around at the many doors to the room and thinking of how he didn't want to see anything come through them.

The two archers thought exactly the same thing and knew what the big guy meant. They fired off a series of well-placed arrows, skewing one through the edge of each door into the jamb, leaving the door toward Dolph's cabin the only one left usable.

Aiden recognised the room immediately, though he'd never entered it from this direction. This was the dining room Santa had brought him into on the first day, arriving in panic and confusion, having just witnessed his sister getting kidnapped by the monster he now knew as Krampus. Also, having discovered Santa was a real person, and the elves were too, which was all explained to him as he sat down to that magical breakfast. It was the same room, but the elvish pride and perfection were very much removed and destroyed. The beautiful big table was snapped in half, with thick splinters sticking up like skewers. The tall-backed chairs had been thrown across the room like discarded rubbish, snapped into pieces, with a few smashed right into the formerly beautiful wallpaper.

'Keep moving.' Santa went on, and he walked quickly across the room. Sophie skipped her little legs into a jog as she tried to keep up. Her fear of being captured again preventing any chance of falling behind. Aiden marched along by her side, but he had now taken on a different role. He wasn't just the kid being taken along for a ride, fearing for his little sister. No, he had decided it was time to become the fighter Dan trained him to be; a warrior, part of the team, one of the elves.

Rushing through Dolph's front door at the end of the next long straight corridor with the right mix of urgency and caution, they found the place disturbed and shaken, but still elfishly so. Rushed and panicked rather than vandalised and smashed. There were signs of mess and panic, yet it was an ordered one, not a mess of attack and destruction, but of hurried movement out of there by many sets of feet.

The group came to a quick halt at the doorway, with the first couple running into Santa's big red back as he stood on the threshold to the living room, looking around the place very carefully.

'This is good. Only elves have been through here.' he declared with certainty, then stepped across the floor to where a dark green set of puffy lounge chairs sat neatly in the corner with a chunky dark timber coffee table sat in the space in front of them. Fitting in with what was the expected standard of elves, it was carefully crafted. The joints in the timbers locked together tightly and with surgical precision, the edges rounded off into a waving curve that flowed into the detailed floral carvings bordering the top of the table. On it sat one very old coffee-stained mug. Santa reached for the mug, leaving more than just Aiden wondering why Santa would think this was a good time to drink whatever was left in the old orange crockery. He took hold of its handle, a little tighter than one would normally grab a coffee, and he pulled it. Turning the whole thing with a metallic click, he twisted this coffee cup dial to open, and the floor shook as it began to move. The table, the coffee cup, and the whole section of floor under it, all lifted slightly, then slid away from where they stood stunned in the doorway. It opened to show a stairwell below.

More of the same timber from the floorboards had been used down here for the stairs, though it was all a little simpler, serving a function, installed with skill but without any unnecessary fancy bits. A round, matt black handrail followed the stairs down on each side, and dull but adequate lights were strung up from the raw ceiling above, with the stairs coming to a landing a short way below, and changing into a level hallway which went quite a way into the mountain.

'Dan, lead the way,' Santa said, stepping to the side and waving him past, then stopped Blitz as he went to follow him in. 'You're up here with me, mate.'

'What do you mean? Aren't you coming?' Dan stopped to ask, concerned by what the alternative might mean.

'Just keep going. Take these two through to the others, then come back up. We'll wait and guard against anyone that comes. We need them safe first, then we'll go hunting for Krampus.' he said with a dangerously serious look in his eyes.

Dan nodded and took off, with his hurried steps

drumming on the timber steps, telling Aiden as nicely as he could to shut up and move when he protested he should be staying up top to help fight.

24

Just like the vision that greeted their friends a little earlier, the team of elves on the river saw the thick, black columns of smoke rising above their home. Dash, Vick, Coop, Comet and Donny were past the furious wash of the rocky sections that were so determined to knock them around, and were now in the steadier, but still fast-moving, final stretch to home. Home. They wondered what would be left as the turn of each bend brought more destruction into sight.

It was an odd sensation, Dash thought to himself as he sat on his now slightly smaller chunk of ice, leaning his back against the vertical handle of his sword. This rather peaceful drift, which they had no control over, through some otherwise quite beautiful scenery, was in total contrast to the scenes at their home a few miles ahead, and the madness he knew waited for them.

'I don't know what we're about to walk into down here, but it doesn't look good,' Vick began, looking around the group but they all knew she was addressing Dash who tried to quickly reply with something to lift morale, and she spoke over him with 'My point is that if we keep going like this and just drift around the bend by the bridge, we'll have no chance – nowhere to hide and unable to run – mere target practice.'

Only two bends in the river to go, and very little time, they all quickly agreed they should make their way onto land before that last bend. They could then take the somewhat concealed path along the river's edge where a reasonably thick row of trees would provide something to hide behind.

Donny was closest to the edge and jumped high enough to get a grip on a low-hanging branch, from which he could pull himself up and out before working to fish his friends across to the bank with long sticks and vines.

The numbing cold was replaced by a pleasant spring warmth, which came suddenly this time of year, with the pink and white flowers decorating the trees.

'Come on, let's go. We'll get a good look at the place from the little rise in the path at the edge of the farm.' Dash said, pointing out what they all already knew, as he led the way.

They followed the path along the bank with the river on their right, and the last of the forest on the left. They marched along at an enthusiastic pace, desperate to see their precious home, and their friends hopefully doing well in its defence.

It hit them like a blow to the heart as they stepped over the rise and looked across the burning fields; The Pole, devastated and crawling with trolls and other monsters under Krampus' control.

'We're too late.' Vick sobbed as the tears lined her cheeks.

'There's trolls everywhere, there must still be elves inside, they couldn't possibly have gotten out.' Comet added.

'What are we going to do?' Vick asked in a barely

audible squeak, as more of a statement of hopelessness than a real question.

No one said anything for a moment as they all expected Dash to come out with some calming wisdom, which he did not. Coop spoke. 'We're going to get in there and find our friends. That's what we're going to do.'

'Santa didn't come racing back to just lose a fight. They're in there somewhere, and they are fighting hard. They need our help.' Donny added, and when no response came, particularly from Dash, who they really needed right now, he walked over and shook him sharply.

'Wake up, Dasher.' he blasted, a little louder than he felt he needed to.'I'm sorry, I'm sorry, yes, you're right, we need to help them. It's not too late.' Dash spat out quickly, looking around the group. He switched back on now and moved over against the log with Coop, instructing the others to follow, and took a few minutes to have a more thorough look over the chaos, analysing what was happening.

'Alright,' he started after looking and thinking quietly to himself for a moment, 'Let's keep moving down to the bridge; after that, the trees end and we're in the open, but we can get a better look from there before we let ourselves be seen.' he finished, and started walking again down the path immediately, not waiting for questions, and thinking only of the urgency of their actions and how crucial the timing of their arrival might be to the survival of the elves.

Stress and worry were not reduced at all when they looked over the madness from their last point of hiding. They looked out and saw many more trolls than any of them had expected; hundreds of them. They were right in around the building, where they looked to be about to enter, breaking anything in their path. The small group of elves were watching this in horror, watching their precious home being vandalised, pointlessly and stupidly, as many of the trolls seemed to have no idea what they were doing, or why. Then something distracted them and took their attention to the mountain on the far side of it all.

'Dolph.' Dash yelled without thinking as he recognised his dear old friend miles away, riding up the mountain with someone he feared to be Krampus, chasing him.

'Oh Dash.' Coop cursed under his breath at his friend, who instantly realised his error. The yell had thick, ugly troll heads turning their way, and many of them taking their first steps toward them.

25

'Yeah, my fault,' he apologised. 'Let's go. We need to get to the mountain side of the trolls before they reach us.' he explained, pointing from the charging trolls to Dolph, following his suggested route through the paddocks along the river as they ran.

'What about the rest of the elves inside?" came Vick.

Dash looked toward the trolls and saw almost every one of them were now turning their attention to them, and replied, 'They're all coming after us now, the elves inside have nothing to worry about.'

They ran as fast as they could, which was not all that fast under various levels of exhaustion, and they had a long way to go. Though trolls are certainly stupid, they were coming from all different directions around the place, so it seemed certain they would cut off the elves' path before they could position themselves to help Dolph.

As the elves tired, the trolls got closer and the little group were steeling themselves for an unwinnable fight.

'It's either fight several hundred trolls or jump back in the water.' Vick suggested pointing to the river, not giving them any chance against the trolls.

'Fight.' Donny replied stubbornly as he tightened the grip on his sword and the group slowed slightly, like they all felt the futility of trying to outrun them.

'No, no, keep going, there's another option. Run.' Coop said, pushing them to run faster again as he pointed over through the paddocks to where a group of reindeer were charging their way, ploughing through anything in their path like roadkill.

A miniature, and very brief, celebration came and went as they realised it wasn't over yet. The first of the trolls were uncomfortably close now, and the elves were all looking over their shoulders at the charging reindeer and urging them on with shouts of encouragement and high-pitched whistles, when Dash noticed something. 'There's someone riding them.'

'It's Santa!' Coop yelled, puffing for breath, with the joy and relief in his words obvious.

'And Dan and Blitz.' Dash added, and looked around the rest of the pack, but they were the only three with passengers. After leading Aiden and Sophie down the tunnel and finding the rest of the elves, Dan had gone back up to Santa and Blitz, leaving Rance to stand guard. They were surprised to find no trolls at all waiting to fight them, and hundreds charging up the hill after their friends. Then the reindeer came running to help.

They galloped in beside the sprinting elves, and Santa threw an open hand out toward Dash with a look that told of the happy relief at seeing him arrive in good health. Dash took the big baseball glove-sized hand and was thrown through the air onto the back of the next reindeer, taking hold of its antlers as he drew a weapon. The reindeers' heads dropped as they ran, offering antlers to the rest of the elves, which they took hold of and were flipped up onto the thick furry backs without missing a step, and they were now winning the race for position to defend Dolph, accelerating away from the trolls.

'Is everyone alright?' Dash shouted over the rumble of hooves and fat troll feet as elves exchanged greetings.

'Yeah, nothing a bit of rest and a good feed won't fix.' Santa replied.

'And the kids?'

'They're heading through the tunnels under the mountain with the rest of the elves right now. They're fine.'

'Excellent. And have you got hold of Krampus yet?' Dash asked, hoping they had already won some small battle.

'No, that's him up there chasing Dolph.' Santa said, pointing up the mountain.

'Yeah, that's not good.' Dash said under his breath. 'Can Dolph beat him?' he asked doubtfully.

Santa looked across to Dash with a grim face. 'Very unlikely. I mean, there was a time, but not at his age. And he would know that, but he's just trying to lead Krampus away long enough and use any magic he can to hurt him while everyone else gets to somewhere safe.'

'Of course.' Dash conceded with a roll of the eyes.

'Classic Dolph, cares too much about everyone else and not enough about himself.' Coop added, overhearing the conversation.

'Yeah, we've got to get up there.' Dash agreed.

'No, I'll get up and help him defeat Krampus; you lot just stop them from following.' Santa said, pointing at the trolls with a short sword.

'That's a big ask mate.' Dash observed, looking around at

the sea of trolls and dragons moving in a long wave toward them, threatening to pull them in and just smother them.

'There could be ten or twenty times our number on their side. I mean, we'll do all we can, but the fact is we won't hold them back for long. If at all.'

'You're right, but if we can get up onto the rocky section, amongst the boulders on that ledge,'"" he explained, trying to put the idea of hope into their heads, 'They could, maybe, be at least slowed down. They won't be able to climb up easily, not the trolls, and they will be easy targets as they try.'

'I don't know mate.'

'Have you got a better idea?' Santa snapped, knowing they didn't have time to argue.

'No, none at all actually.'

'Well, trust me Dasher, I think this is our best chance. We have to go for it, and I need you to take the lead for me.' came the plea from Santa, desperate for his unofficial deputy to support him. The reindeer accelerated up the slope toward the rocky cliffs.

'Alright mate, we'll hold them back. You just make sure you bring Dolph back.' Dash agreed with a look that reminded Santa he would be there to support him whatever the situation, and the big, bearded man yelled at his reindeer and charged away from his friends, toward Dolph and the monster nearing the top of the mountain.

Passing a short steep section on the path, Dash saw a few things that gave him an idea as he passed through an opening between two pieces of stone and stopped, turning on the spot. 'Get some reindeer behind here and push these over.' He said, directing a couple of them in to push the road-block into place, while Dan and Blitz stood ready to put an arrow into anything that arrived first.

With a few puffing reindeer grunts and slip of a few hooves, the tall stone pieces fell with a loud thump, closing the path and leaving the series of small cliffs around the corner as the only option for the trolls. With the power of the elevated position of these little cliffs, and a few clusters of large round rocks providing some shelter to shoot from, Santa was right, and now Dash knew it; they were a real chance at holding this army back, and he turned to watch up the mountain as Santa disappeared from view.

26

Dolph knew the elves were safe for now, deep in the tunnels beneath the mountain, but that would only last as long as he could keep Krampus distracted, or take him out completely. But was that possible? It was a fight he didn't look forward to, but he was daring to fantasise about it happening. If everything went his way, perhaps it was possible. The trolls didn't concern him too much; he knew they were far too stupid to ever find the tunnels, given any length of time.

'You may as well just stop old man.' Krampus yelled up the hill at the elvish wizard in his gravelly voice that sounded like it could burst into a coughing fit at any moment.

Dolph continued until he reached the apex of the mountain, then turned to look back down the path. 'Run out of places to hide?' the beast grunted when he got a few dozen metres from the old elf.

Dolph ignored the question. 'Why'd you come back?' he said.

Krampus looked around the view over the valleys, admiring it like it was his, and smiled slightly as he looked down, almost laughing to himself. 'Come back? Right.' he mumbled, then spoke up and responded, 'I never left. I never stopped; I just chose my targets a little more carefully for a while.'

Dolph stared back at him without speaking, trying to read his face, searching for signs of this being either truth or a lie. It couldn't be true. They couldn't have lost all those lives without knowing. Could they?

'No. Why? Why change?' Dolph challenged him.

'Why? Are you serious?' Krampus replied, then went on without allowing time for a response. 'Because I'm not as stupid as you elves think I am, that's why. With every Christmas Eve attack, as you know, as the story goes, I have grown with power, and to this point I'm no longer threatened by your hero Santa.' he explained, exaggerating the word hero in a mocking tone and a distorted face, and continued, 'So here I am, and if he wants to protect the world from me, come and protect it.' He escalated to a rough scream by the end, and he picked up a rock nearly the size of Dolph's whole body and threw it at him with a burst of energetic rage.

The elf stepped to the side, away from the flying rock with relative ease, drawing his wand as he went and holding it at his hip, gripping his sword with the other, ready for whatever may come next. Krampus wasn't trying to hit him with the rock. There was no thought given to aim at all. It was more a show of strength and a loss of temper.

'So, you've been sneaking around like a cowardly wolf picking the wandering sheep from the edges of the flock, trying to avoid being noticed by that which you have always feared and trying to avoid Santa?'

'No. That right there is the mistake you lot make. There's a significant difference between fear and intelligence; in knowing yourself and your opponent, and what I do know is my power has grown, and Santa's just the same old boring, predictable man who's stopped growing, stopped developing, and is nothing to me.' Krampus shouted arrogantly as if Santa may be in earshot.

'Someone as intelligent as you're claiming to be wouldn't underestimate this old wizard though, would he?' Dolph snapped back with blank faced attitude as he adjusted himself, feeling a fight was close.

The big, powerful villain paced about across the track, still coming gradually closer to the elf, and tore a stone chunk off a boulder with his right hand and threw it like a baseball, hard. This time it was very much aimed straight at Dolph's head, but he never anticipated the old wizard's reflex to counter it.

Having expected something, he was ready, and with his wand in his hand, he quickly had it up in front of him, stopping the stone missile right in front of his face. After hanging there in space under a wave of his wand for a tiny piece of a second, it snapped back at Krampus like it was on an invisible rubber band and shot directly into his big flat forehead.

He stumbled back a step or two and tripped on his own feet, before steadying himself and roaring with anger as he rubbed the embarrassing sore spot.

Dolph was initially pretty happy with himself, and relieved he still had it in him, having not used these skills for a long time. Then he heard the rage in Krampus' scream, which vibrated right through him, as the beast took the first steps toward him and drew an intimidating weapon, leaving the elf wondering whether it was wise to make him mad.

Santa shook and looked up as he heard the horrible roar, and could not mistake its source, or what it meant. He pushed the reindeer on with all the urgency there was.

Krampus charged up at Dolph, shrinking the small distance between them, and swinging his six-foot-long axe as he went. Again, it was like a temper tantrum, but this time with focus, as he smashed chunks of rock off with the back of his weapon, painfully spraying it at Dolph.

Dolph raised an arm, covering his face with his thick green coat, then quickly realised blinding himself like this for the sake of protection could be a big error, and he swung back around to look at his attacker, blasting back as he turned. The rush, and perhaps lack of magical practice, had him miss sending the spray of rock back at the beast, and all he managed was a blast of dirt and dust up toward his face.

It wasn't what was intended, and the cloud was thick and heavy, totally blinding both of them. Dolph knew he was in trouble instantly. He now had a blinded monster launching at him through brown nothingness. Bang, they collided.

Dash rolled over the moment he hit the ground and orientated himself. He pulled into an alert squat, looking around and rubbing his eyes as he searched. He knew he was knocked through the air for what felt like a long way, but where was Krampus? Was he close? Was he even on his feet? Or maybe he ran himself off the cliff behind them, Dolph hoped.

He felt the presence of the beast through the dust before he knew where he was. He just somehow knew he was close. Spinning in a tight circle as he backed away, while not really knowing which direction away was, he bumped right into him like he was one of the big stone cliffs. The old elf felt an impossibly thick and muscular arm wrap around his neck, and he knew any breath he took now could be his last if the arm was to so much as flex slightly.

The jarring feeling shook him as the huge body smacked hard into him and would have sent the smaller than average elf flying if not for the choke hold that stopped him. His instinctive response was to break Krampus' hold with magic, as he was never going to overpower him physically, but his left hand was now empty. No wand. It must have been knocked onto the ground. His right hand was still gripping his sword tight, but the control of it had been taken, with the hard and rough hand of Krampus completely covering his, clamping it to the grip at his hip.

'The part of the story that talks about the attacks increasing my power has already proven true; look at me. My power growing by the year, by the crime. But my first wizard, this is a big moment for me, and for history.' Krampus boasted loudly, directly into Dolph's ear, squeezing him so close he could feel the beast's heart thumping through the layers of armour.

'You're going to kill me for that?' he gasped.

'Oh, I am. The legendary Rudolph. I'm looking forward to this.' he finished.

'You can't take my power just by killing me, Krampus. You just can't, that's not how it works.' The elf continued trying to convince him.

'So, you're saying the rest of it is true, the proof of which is holding you at death's driveway right now, but the part of this prophecy that requires you to die just happens to be a lie? How perfectly convenient for you.' Krampus mocked.

'No, all I'm saying is it doesn't work like that.' Dolph started, thinking fast for an idea to extend his life by just a few more seconds, as he had just heard the familiar sound of reindeer hooves, and correctly assumed it meant Santa was close. 'A wizard's power can't be transferred at his death without his wand in his hand. The magic is in neither the wizard nor the wand alone but exists only with the two as one. It is simply dissolved when a wizard dies without it.' he finished.

For a second Krampus didn't seem to believe him, and Dolph thought his head was going to pop right off as the arm around his neck tightened while the thought was turned over in the monster's mind.

'Where is it, you stupid elf?'

'What?' Dolph squeaked out in response.

'The damn wand.'

Dolph pointed down toward his feet through the dust cloud that still hung in the air and kicked a foot out toward it. 'There, on the ground.' he spoke.

Krampus released the hold from around his neck and bent down to get the wand himself, keeping a grip on the hand which held the sword, not thinking there was any risk in doing so. Then, with a skittling bam and a hard thump, Santa arrived.

27

He crashed in, sending them all rolling to the ground in random directions like a set of pins scattered by an angry bowling ball. The wisdom and experience of Dolph had him set on making sure his wand was back in his hand, and as soon as he picked it up, he used it to blast that thick wall of dust away and into the sky above them.

The three of them now stood in the clear on top of the mountain. 'Oh ok.' Krampus said, in a strange almost laughing rhythm. 'I deserved that. I've underestimated you people before.'

The dust moved into the sky above, and the mountain top became still. Krampus moved his sight between the relieved looking Dolph and Santa, who stood tall, his heart beating fast as he looked back at Krampus without fear. Krampus shook his head, disappointed in himself for letting the fight reach this point and not ending it earlier. He should have finished it while it was just him and the pathetic old elf, he thought.

Santa and Dolph both watched him very carefully as he stood looking at the two of them in quiet thought, and then suddenly, and quiet unexpectedly, he stepped toward Dolph. 'Alright, let's get this over with.' he griped.

Santa was standing only a couple of metres from the old wizard, and from the time Krampus made his first move, he was taking a stance in front of his friend within a second or two. Krampus raised his long axe and pointed it toward Santa's face. 'You're nothing to me.' he hissed aggressively.

Santa just stood and watched as Krampus charged at them. Then when he was a few metres away, put a handout behind him and shoved Dolph back, and threw himself forward into the fight.

The two giant warriors collided like a couple of wild buffalo battling over a piece of territory, with a loud skull shaking smack. Both were shaken but neither backed off, exchanging blows of weapons before coming to a fist fight wrestle on the rocky ground.

As they became tired, losing all sense of how long the fight had been going, blood began to drop from them both as they each tried to ignore the pain of their injuries. The great skills and training of Santa were overwhelmed by the superior size and strength of Krampus as they both became more tired and the struggle for a winning position continued. The beast began to feel he would be taking another life soon.

Santa fought and struggled, and unable to overpower the monster or wrestle himself free, his mind moved to Dolph. He only hoped the old wizard had used this time to escape. To get as far away from there as he could. To find a way to stay alive.

But he had not. He moved on Krampus and connected a

hard swing of his sword right into the side of him, breaking the armour at his right shoulder open and hurting him. The beast fell to the ground and held the wound, sending Santa rolling away from him as he fell, and turned, glaring up at the elf, furious.

He stood up, picked up his weapon again, and moved to attack Dolph, grabbing him and wrestling him to the ground.

'All you did was delay this moment slightly, old wizard. You can't stop me.' Santa heard the gravelly, rough voice say and forced himself to his feet again. He stumbled across, under the pain of his injuries, and kicked at his nemesis, knocking him off the elf.

He bent down and took Dolph's hand, hoping to get him onto the reindeer that he himself had come on, and get him away, but Krampus was back up. He reached for the sword on the ground by Dolph, and the elf saw his opportunity. He raised his wand and recited the curse he knew was the only one for this horrible beast, and a struggle for control was already on. Krampus wrapped one hand around the elf's forearm, trying to point the wand away to miss him. Santa dived on them, lunging his hand over Dolph's, overpowering Krampus and pointing the wand directly at his horrible face, but no spell came. No magic, no killer blast.

Dolph dropped to the ground limp, impaled on Krampus' weapon. Dead.

Krampus got to his feet and stood over Santa, who held his dear friend's body. He didn't know in that moment whether he had in fact been hit by a spell at all. He thought he'd seen a flash of brightness as he lunged the sword forward with a rush of adrenaline, then the ecstasy of this long-pursued success as he felt the relief of his reward rush through him.

With Dolph dead and Santa aching with grief, Krampus

walked away slowly toward the cliff and just stepped off. He was gone.

The trolls had realised pretty quickly they had no chance of getting past the elves at the base of the mountain, and lost interest, leaving the elves free to come up and help. With no idea of what had just happened, or the terrible tragedy they were about to discover, they came walking up over the crest to the sight of Krampus flying away on a large black dragon, and Santa bent over the dear old elf on the ground, the legendary Rudolph.

'Dolph!' came the shouts from down the path as the elves saw the scene on top of the mountain and knew the worst had happened.

'No.', 'Rudolph.', 'No, no, no.', 'How could this happen.' The cries continued.

The group of elves arrived at their side and Santa looked up at them with tears in his eyes, heartbroken, disappointed, and angry. 'He's gone.' he said quietly.

They gathered around the great wizard in a circle, wrapping their arms around Santa, and they all dropped their heads and just sat quietly for a moment.

'You did all you could Santa. And I'll tell you this for certain, we're going to find Krampus for this, and he's finished. Even with the stolen elvish magic, when we find him, he's going to wish he was never born.' Dan said angrily in a shaky voice.

Santa raised his head and looked around the group, making eye contact with each one of them, then looked down at his hand, still wrapped around Dolph's hand and the wand. 'The elvish magic didn't transfer to Krampus; it came to me.' he said, and he knew, as did all the elves, Dolph's final act had saved them all. With that power, Krampus would have been unstoppable. But now, Santa had the power to protect the world, fight off Krampus and any other evil that may come, and continue Dolph's pet side project as the Christmas delivery guy.

Shawline Publishing Group Pty Ltd
www.shawlinepublishing.com.au

9 781922 594273